Praise for

Red Dog Conspiracy

"The author creates vivid scenes and complex characters and a plot that keeps you turning the pages."

— COLLEEN MOONEY

"The author is an amazing storyteller, all of the characters are well written where you can imagine them as existing in real life, they have flaws and some are more likable than others. These books are fantastic and I can't wait for the next one ..."

— ALEXANDER C. DESTIN

"Crime families. Corruption. Kidnapping. Murder. Betrayal. What more could a reader ask for ...?"

— CHERIE JUNG, Over My Dead Body

"... a mystery story of the first order in the best tradition of Sherlock Holmes."

— CLABE POLK

"I love the sympathetic characters Loofbourrow creates. She crafts them slowly and carefully, building to an inexorable crescendo that pulls out all the emotional stops. They are ones that others tend to overlook, just extra names to fill in background roles— until time calls upon them to rise to the occasion, and then they are swept up into a frenzy of peril and intrigue that threatens to devastate them, or bolster them into heroic acts."

— LESLIE CONZATTI, Upstream Writer

"... definitely worth the read for those who love a good mystery."

— UNCAGED BOOK REVIEWS

For more reviews, see JacqOfSpades.com

BOOKS BY PATRICIA LOOFBOURROW

RED DOG CONSPIRACY

The Jacq of Spades

The Queen of Diamonds

The Ace of Clubs

The King of Hearts

The Ten of Spades (coming October 2019)

THE PREQUELS

The Alcatraz Coup

Gutshot: The Catastrophe

Vulnerable

THE COMPANIONS

Drawing Thin

DRAWING THIN

A Companion to the Red Dog Conspiracy

Patricia Loofbourrow

Published by Red Dog Press, LLC

Printed in the USA

1

Constable Paix Hanger had attended many crime scenes, yet something about this one unnerved him. No blood splattered the empty alley, no bodies adorned the back rooms of this sad little fabric shop.

That was the problem, he decided.

The boy was just — gone.

He closed his notebook, putting it and his pencil into his pocket. The room was odd. He'd seen similar rooms before, this close to the Pot — minimal battered furnishings, nothing on the walls — but this room held an emptiness that pulled at his heart.

No smell of food. No personal items lying about. Not even a toy or doll on the boy's thin mattress.

Paix considered himself at that age. The boy was twelve, even if he looked ten, perhaps too old for dolls. But not even a book?

Forensics men dusted the open back door frame and back stair railing for fingerprints while others photographed the barren room and the child's portrait. The family peered in from the doorway to their storefront, following the officers' every move. The mother — in her middle forties with dark eyes and hair — and a young man of sixteen, who looked like her. Their clothes were well-made, too fine for a 2nd Street address.

Probationary Constable Leone Briscola stood in front of them, arms on the door-posts, blocking the way. "You think he ran off?"

Paix flinched at the outrage which flashed through the mother's eyes. This would make things more difficult. He gave Briscola a sharp stare. "We don't have enough evidence to say anything yet."

Briscola's swarthy cheeks reddened, his dark eyes dropping at the rebuke.

Paix strode to the open back door. Clouds covered the late December sky, yet Lady Luck had smiled upon them — it was mid-morning, with little chance of rain. Cases like these at night in a thunderstorm were much more difficult.

From the narrow steps, Paix had a clear view of the entire alley. A team photographed the alley, while another collected every item in it — trash, half-eaten rats, bits of wood — each placed into its own brown paper sack, the top folded and sealed. Labelled. Catalogued.

If this were any other precinct, a detective or three would be ordering them around. But Precinct 1 was stretched too thin for that luxury. Their job was to do the preliminaries. Whatever detective was assigned would follow up on the case tomorrow.

The alley wall across the way looked like any other. Paix moved close to inspect it: graffiti, but no hairs, no fibers, nothing to speak of what happened here.

They should have cordoned off the entire alley, and examined the back stair first. Dozens of officers had walked these stairs, and others had trailed through the alley while they spoke with the family inside. "Photograph every shoe-print of every man here. And the family's."

"Yes, sir."

It was routine, but he didn't want to leave anything to chance. Those eyes in the boy's tintype portrait haunted him.

Paix pointed to a fresh mark — a dog, stamped in red on the grimy brick wall. "Did you photograph this?"

"Yes, Constable, but it won't help much." The photographer, a slender, curly-haired man dark as a Diamond, shook his head regretfully. "Colors don't show with this film. I called for an artist."

Paix continued down the alleyway. No signs of a struggle suggested the boy knew his kidnapper — or was lured away. He turned to face his team.

Briscola stood facing him. "They're done with the room."

"Don't ever make a determination in front of the family."

Briscola's cheeks reddened. "Sorry, Constable."

Paix kept his voice low. "Sorry won't mend this. It's bad

enough most of the force is on the take, or shaking down people for crossing the street wrong, or playing target practice in the Pot. You know how rare it is for someone to actually call us the day of a crime?" He turned away, trying to keep his anger under control. Then he faced his partner. "You're a good cop. But you have to keep your mouth shut. Understand?"

Briscola's head drooped. "Yes, sir."

Paix clapped Briscola's shoulder. "What do you see?"

The young man's face steadied, his shoulders straightened.

It was encouraging. He hoped Briscola would survive.

"No signs of a struggle, sir. Nothing of his left at the scene. The family heard no noise —" Briscola turned to Paix, astonished. "The boy didn't cry out."

"Notice anything else?"

"Last night was Yuletide Center. Where are the decorations? The food? The gifts?"

Paix nodded. And the rest of her family. Where were they?

Good thing I was assigned this case, he thought. This woman was barely surviving. To have to choose between bribes and food .... "What else?"

He watched as Briscola struggled to find something, anything to say. Finally, Briscola shook his head.

"The mother. She's hasn't given her children a Yuletide, yet still wears a wedding ring."

Briscola's eyes unfocused, blinked several times. Then he frowned, his mouth twisting. "She loves her children. It's not that." He hesitated. "Recently widowed?"

She took off her mourning garb, yet she kept her ring. "Yes, and by the look of things, newly arrived to Bridges." The answer came to him in a flash. "They're running from something."

* * *

The officers returned to the house, and Mrs. Bryce offered them tea. As there were only three stools, the young man — Herbert was his name — lounged on his bed, watching in silence.

That they were offered tea seemed encouraging. Perhaps she'd speak more of her troubles.

Paix said, "Was this your first voyage on the zeppelin?"

"No, sir," Mrs. Bryce said stiffly. "We've traveled before."

Her accent seemed familiar but he couldn't place it. "Did you enjoy your trip here?"

They both flinched.

He decided to try a different approach. "Mrs. Bryce, what brought you to Bridges?"

She glanced away. "I had opportunity to own a business."

He peered at her. She hid something. Why? "Anything you can tell us might help."

The woman glanced at her son. "We owed money. Back in Dickens. We — I thought we'd be safe here."

Paix nodded. Now he recognized the accent.

Financial refugees from Dickens were not unheard of. A dollar from Dickens was a small fortune in the slums of Bridges. "But why come **here**?" Fees from the local crime family, outrageous rents with little in return — this wasn't the best play for a gentlewoman in financial distress.

She glanced away. "This was where opportunity lay." She faced him, then set her teacup down, her manner formal. "Will there be anything else?"

Something wasn't right here.

He handed her his card. "Madam, I'm here neither for your money nor your favors. We want to be of service. But I don't want to further impose on you. If you think of anything which might be helpful, or if anyone contacts you about the boy, or if your son returns, please let us know."

Her cheeks reddened, but she stood: it was time for them to leave.

* * *

The men in the alleyway were packing their gear, but gave Paix their attention when he emerged.

"I want a door-to-door search in a six-block radius," Paix said. "Four of you come with me: we'll take the Pot. The rest finish packing then split into teams." He counted quickly, then pointed to one of them. "You stay here and watch the house in case the boy returns." He raised his voice to encompass them all. "Each team take search bags. Play it straight, men. The boy is here somewhere, and the clock is ticking." If the child were taken, as the mother seemed to think, every minute which passed without finding David Bryce left less hope of him being found alive.

And he'd been gone several hours already.

Paix and his group strode to the corner, then turned towards the Hedge. David Bryce might have gone to some neighbor's house, invited in with warm food and gifts. But the Bryce family had been in Bridges only a short time; his mother insisted she knew of no friends here.

Paix peered up and down the intersection before crossing 1st Boulevard. This didn't feel right. If his hunch were true — the family was indeed running from someone — the boy would feel anxious, wary of strangers. He wouldn't have left home without telling his mother.

Yet he didn't cry out. Why?

They crossed the wide, broken-down boulevard to one of the gaps in the Hedge, then the group slipped through.

Paix shuddered, the hair on his arms rising. They had crossed into the Pot.

"You two," he pointed to his right. "up three. You two," he pointed to his left, "up five. Six blocks to each side. Meet back at the wagons when you're done."

The men shifted a bit with sour faces, especially the ones asked to go six blocks into the Pot. But Paix had no qualms they would follow. He waited until they deduced his reasoning: he was senior, and had a new Probationary with him. They nodded, and set off.

Paix was within his rights to order, to bluster, to demand. But he never liked to work that way. Men who understood and agreed meant men who'd follow orders — and come back alive.

The six men crept straight across the empty wide street paralleling the Hedge. Then they moved forward, one silent step at a time, nightsticks drawn, keeping to the center of the street. Broken glass lined the gutters, in places ground fine as sand. On either side, the bombed-out ruins stood eerily quiet.

At the first intersection, Paix and Briscola stopped, while the other men pressed on. Paix whispered to Briscola, "Have you been in the Pot before?"

Briscola shook his head, face pale. The paper sack in his hand made a crinkling noise.

"They will try to kill you if they can."

A whistle rang out, high and to the left. Briscola jumped at the sound. The rest, several yards ahead, didn't even flinch.

Paix shouted with full force. "A boy's gone missing. We need your help."

Silence lay heavy in the air. Then across the street to their left, a boy emerged from a battered yet elaborately carved corner door. The boy was seven years old and blond, wearing the bright red jacket of his trade.

Two older boys, twelve or so with light brown hair, followed, the familiar bulge of a weapon at each boy's side.

Briscola let out a loud breath.

Paix relaxed, yet kept watchful. "Greetings, Memory Boy."

"Good morning, Constables."

Memory Boys remembered everything: heard, seen, or written. Paix thought this might be a curse rather than a blessing, although the families of these children lacked for nothing. "What have you heard of a boy missing?"

"Nothing," the Memory Boy said. "What's he like?"

Paix peered around. They were much too exposed. "Let's get out of the street."

The older boys nodded; the group moved back against a wall. Far off ahead, two Constables turned right, their motions wary.

"Briscola, watch the windows." Paix crouched to the Memory Boy's height. The boy's companions — from the look if it, his brothers — stood watching everywhere but them. "His name is David Bryce. He's twelve, but small: he looks ten. Just arrived from Dickens. Dark hair and eyes, but light of skin."

"I haven't heard of him," the boy said, "but I'll listen."

"Thanks," Paix said. "And ask the Clubbs to watch as well."

The boy smiled brightly. "However would I do that?"

"This is no game. Someone's after the family, and I don't want the boy taken from the city."

The Memory Boy's face reddened. "I'll take care of it."

The Clubb crime syndicate owned the only way out of this dome: the zeppelin station and by extension, the Aperture. If the boy was taken out of Bridges, the police would need to involve the Feds for permission to pursue him, and no one — least of all the Clubbs — wanted that.

And everyone knew Memory Boys reported the better information straight to the Clubbs. "Good lad." He straightened. "Safe journey."

"You too," the Memory Boy said, and the three children left.

Briscola said, "What now?"

Running across a Memory Boy had been incredibly fortunate. But they still had work to do. "Have you done a search before?"

"In training."

"Then you know what to do."

Briscola took one of the search bags from the paper sack, a fist-sized muslin bag filled with colored chalk dust then tied shut with twine. He tossed it into the middle of the intersection, leaving a bright pink bloom on the grimy cobblestones. "You always go right," Briscola said, as if reminding himself.

Bemused, Paix followed him.

The two men searched the bombed-out buildings, looking under fallen boards, behind broken walls, down fetid basements. Eventually they reached the six blocks, then circled around to search the other side of the street.

No one interfered, for which Paix was grateful.

When they returned to the pink spot, the bag was gone. Stolen, most likely, perhaps to use as a toy, or to color one of their filthy hovels. The two men moved on.

Once they'd searched the six blocks on the other side of this street, they moved to the next. Briscola marked it with a yellow bag this time.

By the time they were finished searching the second street it was well past midday. They returned to Mrs. Bryce's home. The wagons — and the rest of his men — stood waiting.

No one had found anything.

No one would talk with them.
It was business as usual.

2

Spadros quadrant was divided into 8 precincts, each with double the manpower of the number below it. Which seemed odd, considering the closer you came to the Pot, the more crime was generated.

Over the past twenty years, Paix had rolled his way down to Precinct 1, the largest precinct in the quadrant. A place for senior Trainees rotating through for a month before graduation, Probationary Constables who didn't score well on their Entries, drug-addled or alcoholic cops on their way to death in the Pot, and men like him, who just didn't fit.

Precinct 1 police station was at 24th and Snow, just off Spadros quadrant's Main Road. Paix and Briscola went to a nearby street vendor for luncheon.

Paix ate his rice bowl with relish. He hadn't been on a search in a while, and his meager breakfast was many hours in the past.

"I thought I'd find you here, Hanger."

Paix set down his thick paper bowl, lay his chopsticks across it, and turned to the voice. "C.K!" The two men shook hands. "Want to join us?"

Detective Senior Constable Cartas Kanhu was a big, balding, somewhat too hard-drinking man in a three-piece brown tweed suit. "Sure, I'll sit." He plopped a paper plate containing a burger and fries on the round gray table then held out his hand to Briscola. "You must be the new partner."

After a grimace, Briscola took the man's hand. "Not that new."

C.K. laughed his big belly laugh. "Just teasing. I know who you are." He patted Paix on the shoulder and spoke to Briscola. "This is the best cop on the force, and don't you forget it."

Paix smiled, but when someone said that, the question always flashed through his mind: *so why am I a Constable?*

C.K. grinned at him. "You think your job is bad. I got six cases going at once, and I can't go home until I got leads for all of them." He took a bite of his burger, relaxing into the gray wrought-iron chair. "Damn, this actually tastes good. I must be hungry."

Briscola snickered.

Paix knew why he was a Constable. Why he wasn't a detective anymore — why he would never be a detective again. It meant dealing with the many, many deaths in this city.

It meant dealing with the Families.

The thought of letting those — *people* was too kind a word — own him made his stomach turn.

"Are you going to finish that?" Briscola seemed to be a bottomless pit when it came to food.

Paix pushed the bowl over. Grease was beginning to seep through. "Be my guest."

When Briscola went up to get another serving, C.K. said, "Sorry about that."

Paix shrugged. "It's of no consequence."

"You've had it rough. I mean, you were here when I rotated through as a Trainee."

"And now you're Detective Senior Constable."

"Yeah. And you should be Senior Lead Constable by now, or even have Green's job."

Wolff Green was Commander: the man who ran the station. "Maybe I should." He prepared himself for the inevitable line.

"I won't say it, Hanger. I want to, but I won't."

You gotta learn to play the game.

* * *

Inside the station was semi-controlled chaos, day or night: carts of files trundling past, suspects and witnesses being brought in or led out, clerks bringing this or that somewhere. Paix liked it.

His desk was on the ground floor, where Constables and Probationary Constables sat typing like a sea of secretaries. At the moment, more than three-quarters of the desks were empty: most were out on their beats. When receiving a "major case" such as this one, a half-hour was allowed to prepare reports before returning to duty.

The Lead Constables had a ring of desks on the second floor just inside a black metal banister. Each desk faced the back center stair, which was decorated with threadbare red and green ribbon as a nod to the holiday.

The Senior Lead Constable, the heads of the support departments, and the Commander had their own offices on the third floor, with glass windows overlooking from on high.

The Commander's office was the largest, with picture windows spreading over the entire inside front of the narrow building. Commander Wolff Green, a stern, ancient man, stood surveying the room.

After his last round of trouble, Paix had been assigned a desk precisely in the middle of the room. Paix always imagined it was placed so the Commander could keep an eye on him.

A pale yellow folder sat beside his typewriter, containing a single sheet with the messenger's missing person report and the case number, which was printed on the folder's tab. Paix unbuttoned his jacket, hung it on his chair, sat down, opened his notebook, and retrieved three report forms from his file drawer. Paix didn't like to dilly-dally about with paperwork. He preferred to have some chance at getting home on time.

Briscola trailed behind, setting his rice bowl on the desk to the left. "I hate paperwork."

Paix ignored him: filing a report was part of the job. Placing carbon paper between the sheets, he produced three copies: one for his Lead Constable, one for his Senior Lead Constable, and one for the file. Paix saved the best one for the file.

Paix sat for a moment considering, then opened his file drawer. Recommendation for a second search tomorrow, assuming the boy didn't turn up today — that one he clipped to the report going to his Lead Constable. Request a "Keep A Sharp Look-Out For" (KASLOF) notice with a photograph and description of the child, to go to all taxi-carriage drivers, train stations, the zeppelin station, the hospitals, and the morgues. A request for the Clubbs to detain any children between the ages of five and fifteen attempting to leave the city (male or female — it was too easy to disguise a child) until their identities and those with them were verified.

It wasn't that Paix doubted the word of a Memory Boy, but he wanted it documented that he'd made the request. Fortunately, these were all check-the-box forms and could be done in his own handwriting.

The photographer walked up with a large envelope. "Your photos, sir."

Paix looked up at the man, surprised. "That was fast."

"If it were my child," the photographer said, "I'd want these done right away."

"Make a copy for the missing board, if you will."

"Already done."

It wasn't often you got such quick action. "Thank you." At a whim, he stuck out his hand. "Paix Hanger."

"Martin Roberts," the photographer said. "Pleasure to help."

Paix turned the envelope over to open it. Unfortunately, a good man like Roberts would soon be snapped up by a finer precinct. It was the nature of things in Bridges.

Inside the envelope lay copies of the boy's portrait, already labeled with the case number, with photos of the crime scene and evidence: an imposing stack. The drawing of the red mark on the wall was included as well. Paix slid the envelope into the folder, attaching one copy of the portrait photo to his report for the file with a paperclip.

The boy's eyes burrowed into his soul.

Five hours had passed since David Bryce disappeared. Paix turned to Briscola. "You done with your report yet?"

Briscola had his feet up on his desk, eating. He put his feet on the floor. "What?"

"I want your report on my desk tomorrow morning. No excuses." Paix got up, put on his jacket, buttoned it. "Come on, we gotta go."

Paix dropped his reports in the respective message boxes. A glance over at the Missing Board: David Bryce's photo was pinned there with the rest.

Glimpsing the board always left him melancholy: so many children.

* * *

Paix signed out a carriage from the pool and told the driver to make for the bar over on 33 1/3 Street and Scoop Avenue.

The Backdoor Saloon, like everything else in the quadrant, was owned by the Spadros Family.

Leaving the carriage parked on Scoop, Paix and Briscola went inside. A smoke-filled, black-paneled room lay before them, silver glinting here and there at the bar along the back wall. A door past that led to dealings Paix was sure he didn't want to know about. Round black tables edged in silver held only a few people: it was Yuletide, after all.

Mr. Eight Howell, one of the Spadros men assigned to the street, sat smoking cigars with three others. Howell was a short man with a big bushy beard. He glanced up, surprised. "Constable Paix Hanger. It's been a while. To what do I owe the honor?"

"You got a minute?"

He laughed, resting his cigar in an ashtray. "Sure." He went to another table and pulled out a chair. "You boys want anything?"

"No, thank you," Paix said. Not only were they on duty, he couldn't risk being impaired. A place like this could become as dangerous as the Pot on a moment's notice. Paix and Briscola sat across the table from Howell.

"So what can I do for you, Constable?"

Paix said, "A boy's gone missing. You hear anything?"

Howell seemed genuinely surprised. "From around here?"

"2nd Street. But I thought you might've heard something. A new trafficker in town? A smuggling sweep looking for kids?"

Howell frowned. "No. We don't tolerate shit like that in Spadros anymore. The Old Man put a stop to it."

By "The Old Man" Howell meant Roy Spadros, the quadrant's so-called Patriarch. Paix had never seen the man, only his portrait, but he looked — and sounded — like a truly scary fellow.

"Now I got no idea what goes on in the Pot," Howell said.

"Our next stop, unfortunately," Paix said.

Howell pushed his chair away from the table and stood. "I'll ask around."

Paix pushed his hand into a small second pocket he'd sewn inside his right jacket pocket, palming the five dollar bill he kept there for truly urgent matters. Then he shook Howell's hand, transferring the bill to him.

Howell glanced at his palm, keeping it faced towards him, and smiled. "Pleasure doing business with you."

Paix stood, tipped his hat, and left. Five dollars was half his month's salary, but if this got Howell to take a serious interest for the hope of another, it was worth it.

Now he had to figure out where to get a five to replace it.

When they were back in the carriage, Briscola said, "I thought they wouldn't talk to cops."

"They usually won't." It'd taken a long time to get Howell to trust him.

"So why's he helping you?"

Paix leaned back. "I already heard Spadros was cracking down on kid trafficking. So him helping me is of mutual benefit."

"I don't understand."

"I just told him there's a child snatcher in the quadrant. That's valuable information, might even help him gain points with the guy he reports to." He shrugged. "Sounds as if they're finally serious about clearing out the vermin."

"Plus you paid him."

So he had seen it. "Plus I paid him."

Briscola blinked. "Won't his buddies be angry that he's even talking to you? I thought there was some rule or law about talking to cops."

Paix grinned. "Naw. I know all of them."

"How's that?"

Paix jerked a thumb backwards. "I grew up over there."

As far as he knew, his parents still lived at their little house on 30th, three rooms for them and their seven children, now grown. But Paix hadn't seen any of them in twenty years, ever since his father disowned him.

When Paix joined the police force, his father beat him, told him he was a disgrace and a traitor. His older brothers and sisters didn't lift a finger to help.

Everyone said Paix was a strange child. Instead of idolizing the swaggering Associates and their Acey-Deucey beat-down boys like the other children did, Paix admired the police. He liked the crisp blue uniforms with their brass buttons, the sense of rightness about devoting your life to help others.

The reality was very different.

The Bridges police force was full of weak men. Everyone eventually ended up on the take. Party Time, booze, cash, girls — each form of payola depended on the man's weakness.

Paix was determined never to let himself get that way. He refused to be bribed or look the other way — even when he'd been beaten within an inch of his life. He'd never back down on a case just because it involved some mobster. They were men, like him, and they needed to follow the law, like anyone else.

Too bad his superiors didn't feel the same way.

So here he was, in a job a man with a tenth his experience could handle, with the worst beat in the worst precinct in the city.

But growing up in Precinct 1 did have its occasional advantages.

"I grew up off of 98th," Briscola said.

"Yeah," Paix said, amused. "I can tell."

* * *

The carriage entered the Rathole, a gap in the east side Hedge wide enough for a carriage to pass through the wrought-iron fence. First melted by ray cannon during the early hours of the Coup, then sawed larger by enterprising folk looking to increase trade in the early years thereafter, the Rathole was the most popular way into the Spadros quadrant's section of the Pot.

The shadows were beginning to lengthen by the time they got to the Cathedral. The whores living in that magnificent ruin seemed to know everything that went on in the Pot.

Paix ordered Briscola to stay with driver at the carriage, and keep his nightstick ready. He didn't intend to stay long.

Two massive, heavily tattooed men stood guard at the bottom

of cracked steps leading up to a wide entryway missing its doors. The most massive one glared at him. "Not open til dark, copper."

"I'm looking for a missing boy."

"What's he lookin' like?"

Paix wished he'd brought the photo with him. "Dark hair and eyes, round face, light skinned. Looks about ten. An outsider, from Dickens."

The man shook his head. "Not seen him. Not heard a him neither. Outsider boy'd be talked of minute he opened his trap."

Paix had always only spoken to the girls outside. But this was a serious matter. "Can I ask inside?"

He folded his arms. "Not open til dark."

The last thing Paix wanted was to be anywhere near here come nightfall. "I'll be back."

"You want them to talk, bring something to eat."

Paix already knew that.

When he returned to the carriage, Briscola said, "Well?"

"We got here too late." Sometimes if you came early enough, the girls would be out front, and would talk to you for a penny, or a smoke. "Let's get back to the station."

By the time they got back, night was falling. Paix left Briscola to finish his report, telling him he'd be back in an hour, then he caught a wagon home.

Paix lived in a tiny one-room on Market Center. Servants' quarters, really, but once he crossed the bridge from Spadros quadrant over to the island, he felt a weight off his back. He felt safe and free. Which made the cramped accomodations well worth it.

His mother's cousin by marriage had turned in his cards and left the place to her. The day Paix told his mother he planned to sign up as a constable, she got very pale, then brought him the deed to the room. "The man who owns the building is your cousin Bluff's father. You own the room in it. You'll pay part upkeep, if the roof fails or the pipes leak. Other than that, it's yours, free and clear, to do with as you like." She hesitated, then said, "Don't tell your father I gave it to you."

At the time, Paix didn't understand.

She knew what Papa would do, even then.

The room was up four flights of narrow, poorly-lit stairs then down to the very end of the hall. The place was quiet even in the busiest times — most servants were too exhausted by the end of their day to do much carousing. But tonight, most were gone to stay with family for the holidays.

Paix knocked, then used his key. Reina sat at the table, turning to him with a smile like the sunrise, her long, straight black hair flowing around her smooth brown body like water.

She took his breath away, every time he came home to her.

Paix closed the door as she came to kiss him. He gave her a long hug, savoring the feel of her, then kissed her cheek. "I can stay for dinner."

She drew back. "Is it bad?"

Paix loved that he didn't have to tell her it was a case, or explain why he had to leave. She knew all too well how it worked. And she trusted he wouldn't leave unless he absolutely had to. "A boy missing since this morning."

Reina put her hands to her mouth. "Oh, gods." She turned away, her manner brisk. "Don't worry. Dinner's almost ready. It won't take long."

Paix went to where his clothes hung and changed out of his uniform into comfortable house clothing, hanging the uniform to air out. Even though he wouldn't be home long, he couldn't stand to wear his uniform here. This was their place, where he left the job and all that came with it outside.

He slumped into their other chair as she chopped carrots. "How do you feel?"

She glanced over her shoulder at him. "Still a lot of cramping, and some blood, but not nearly so bad as it was."

He felt relieved. "I'm glad."

She put the knife down, turned to face him. "Jake came over."

"What did he want this time?"

"I think someone told him I went to the apothecary. Or he followed me there."

Paix stood. "This has got to stop." He went to her, put his arms around her. "I'm sorry. He shouldn't have come here, especially now. I thought I made that clear last time. I'll talk to him again."

"I don't want any more trouble —"

Paix pulled away, put his hands on her upper arms. "No. He needs to know he can't just come here like this. I won't have it. It's not fair to you, and ... it's not good for him."

She slumped a little. "Gods, Paix, I wish it hadn't happened like it did."

He pulled her to his chest, a deep sadness right where her head lay, and caressed her hair. "I wish that too."

They ate in silence. Paix wished he could take Reina and leave Bridges, go somewhere that wasn't run by criminals. Get married. Have children and a future.

Yet he just gave half his pay to a mobster. He put his fork down, his head in his hands.

"Paix? What's wrong?"

"We're never getting out of here, are we?"

She stretched her hand across to take his, her eyes moist. "All will be well, beloved. Things have to get better." She chuckled then. "It couldn't get much worse."

He looked around the tiny room, the remains of their sparse dinner, her lips pale from the bleeding she'd endured. "Come here." Paix held her gently, a great wave of emotion filling him. *I must not despair.* She'd given up everything for him. "You're right." He kissed the top of her head.

As they sat there together, weariness swept over him. The old siren song returned, as it did every time: *stay with her, rest, lie down.* He'd already had a long day, begun with an hours-long search on foot. Did he really need to go out into the cold darkness and leave her alone?

It was in those moments Paix understood the weakness the other men faced, the pull towards comfort. Towards the quick and the easy.

But he'd given Briscola his word. Paix kissed her forehead quickly then helped her stand. "If I get back before the Plaza closes, I'll buy meat for Krissmiss dinner."

* * *

When Paix returned to the station, Briscola was sitting on the edge of his desk laughing with a group of other cops. "Report's on your desk."

"Good. Let's go."

The Pot was very different at night. Revelers walked the rubbish-strewn streets, lights blazed in the buildings.

The quadrants use these people, Paix thought, then despise them for it.

A large crowd had gathered around the Cathedral's entry, and the two men he'd seen earlier were busy. Two other men and a few boys assisted them, bringing each party in once they'd been checked. A huge shallow wooden box of weapons, neatly lined up, sat on a table beside the stair. Three more boxes were stacked on the ground behind them, the top one full.

Paix didn't approach them at first. He said to Briscola, "What do you see?"

"Busy night."

Rather too busy for Yuletide, Paix thought. Did none of these men have families? "What else?"

"Might be hard to get to talk to someone."

Paix had an instant of regret for leaving Reina, then he shook himself. He couldn't get distracted, not here. Men died that way. "Come on."

As they moved forward, a six year old boy with dark brown skin and curly blond hair glanced at them and ran inside.

Paix approached the men. "Is your mistress available?"

The man who'd spoken to him earlier didn't even glance his way. "Depends on what you want her for."

Exasperated, Paix said, "I want to talk to her about the missing boy."

"She don't know nothing about it."

"Perhaps I should speak to her myself."

"All's well, Benji." A woman's voice, commanding. She stood in the entryway regal, a well-formed brown-skinned woman near his age in a too thin, glistening dress and robe of pale gold which clung to her body around its high points. It was clear she wore nothing underneath.

Paix felt his body respond to the sight of hers, and willed his eyes on her face. Her hair, black with tight curls. Her cynical brown eyes reminded him of someone.

"Come in, constables," she said. "We'll speak."

Paix glanced back at Briscola: the younger man's cheeks were flushed, his mouth parted. "Steady," Paix said. "We have no friends here."

Briscola licked his lips, eyes darting, face pale, and nodded.

Inside was a lobby, leading to a second set of doors, this time on their hinges. A wave of heat struck them as they entered the vast chamber. Tan linen draped the long, wide passageway to eight feet high, the building curving above it to a ceiling several stories up.

One only need use the nose to discern what went on in this establishment. The sounds confirmed it. Here and there, a woman in the same thin, shimmering, clinging sleeveless dress — without a robe — drew back the linen to reveal a narrow cot, neatly made.

Paix handed the paper sack he held containing leftovers from dinner — potatoes and carrots — to a blonde young woman, who took the bag and curtsied low. Her dress, cut to reveal the upper curve of her high breasts, from this angle let them see all the way down to the golden curls below her taut belly.

Briscola let out a soft moan.

Without looking back, Paix whispered, "Get hold of yourself, man. Remember the boy."

The linen stretched on and on. Boys were here too, and girls, much too young to be in such a place. Yet none looked anything like the one they sought.

At last, the linen ended. The robed woman led them up a set of steps which ran the width of the building to a large, flat, raised area with a huge circle of stained glass in the wall above it. She then went to the right, to a room that while smaller, was still quite large: an office, with a desk which wouldn't be out of place anywhere.

Paix laughed in spite of himself.

The woman frowned. "You find the Cathedral of the Blessed

Dealer funny?"

Paix felt abashed when she put it that way. "Forgive me. I never expected a — a desk here."

Amusement spread across her face. "This **is** a business." She glanced at Briscola, speaking as if to a child. "You want a girl to play with?"

Briscola stiffened, face pale. "No. Thank you."

"Or perhaps you want a boy."

Paix felt annoyed. "We're here about a missing child. An outsider. Your men said they described him to you."

She made a dismissive gesture. "I know nothing of it."

"Have you heard someone asking for a boy like this? Someone you had to turn away?"

The woman gave Paix a sharp look. "You think **that** kind took him?"

"We can't afford to rule anything out." The image on the wall flashed into his mind unbidden. "Does a mark of a dog in red stamped onto a wall mean anything?"

This sent her into a moment of pondering, and Paix watched her. She knew something. Would she tell them the truth?

"We in the Pot don't speak with police," she said. "You know why."

Paix nodded. A century of abuse and betrayal bred cold emnity.

"But here, child-harmers earn death. What will you do with this one when you find him?"

"If someone took this child he'll be sent to the Prison. If he's harmed the child," and suddenly, Paix felt that it was so, "then he'd surely hang."

The woman nodded, her head held high. "Then I'll have my men look for signs of him. If he's in the Pot, I'll know."

This is a queen. This desolate place was her queendom.

"Thank you, mum," he said, and her eyes widened even before he bowed. He'd treated her as not only equal, but his superior. Paix didn't know why he did it, but it seemed right.

Then cynicism returned: she believed him to be mocking her. Had he ruined their chances to find the boy?

Her face hardened. "You may leave now."

* * *

Even though Paix stopped by the station to file an updated report, he'd gotten back to Market Center in time to buy the meat, which lay in its wrapping on the outer windowsill, a light snow covering it.

"The Cathedral's a remarkable place," he said as he lay next to Reina. "It's as if the most holy and the most profane came together and ... touched somehow."

Reina smiled at him in the darkness. "My poet."

His face flushed in pleasure at her praise, but he felt troubled. "Children were being sold there. The sight horrified me."

"Can nothing be done?"

Paix sighed, relaxed into her arms. "Too many people want it. The Pot rags claim the children act willingly, but —"

He felt her nod.

"If it's that or go hungry," she said, "there's little choice."

3

Paix rose early, making a thin oat porridge with bits of dried fruit for them both while Reina slept. He arrived at the station before shift change, sitting on a bench outside the building.

The day was overcast, the ground dusted with snow. A bad sign — it would obscure any evidence they'd missed yesterday.

Almost twenty-four hours since the boy's disappearance. Had the night shift found him? Paix had to hope the child still lived.

Chilled, he drew his overcoat around him and went inside. Men gathered in the conference room for the pre-shift briefing; Paix followed them in.

Commander Wolff Green, an ancient man with wisps of white decorating his spotted head, stood in the front of the room flipping through a sheaf of papers. He peered at the papers with rheumy eyes through thick round spectacles.

C.K. ambled by: disheveled, bags under his eyes. A faint smell of alcohol wafted over. Could he possibly be showing up to briefing drunk?.

"Morning," C.K. said. "Heard you got the missing kid."

"Yeah," Paix said. "You in line for the case?"

C.K. grimaced. "Hope not."

"All right, everyone," the Commander said, folding his spectacles away. "Let's make this quick. Congratulations to Constable Paix Hanger for best reports in November. That's six months running."

A spattering of applause, but some glares too. Everyone hated being shown up, especially over paperwork.

It was the sort of backhanded compliment Paix was used to. For all his smiles and talk, the Commander had never forgotten what happened between Paix Hanger and Jake Bower right outside that door. And he'd never forgiven it, either.

Commander Green continued, "Today's KASLOF flyers are in your mail. Hanger, you want to update them on the boy?"

Paix took a step forward, puzzled. The night shift normally did this sort of thing. "A ten — no, twelve year old boy by the name of David Bryce, also called Davey, dark hair and eyes, wearing a white shirt, dark grey pants, cap, and jacket, with black shoes, went missing around eight yesterday morning. Last seen going out of his back door towards the alley near 2nd and Book."

Some murmurs.

"Widowed mother, a sixteen-year-old brother, family arrived from Dickens two weeks ago. No other family or known friends in Bridges. No reason to run away, but from things the mother said I believe they're fleeing someone."

More murmurs.

"We collected evidence, canvassed a six block radius including into the Pot, and sent a request to detain anyone taking children from the city." He grinned at them. "Once in a while, these mobsters are helpful."

Scattered laughter, quickly hushed.

"I've made a few inquiries." He shrugged. "With a Spadros man I know —"

That raised eyebrows. Everyone knew how he felt about the Family.

"— and over at the Cathedral."

A low wolf whistle.

Commander Green glared in the whistle's direction.

"No one has seen or knows anything. As usual." Paix paused for a moment, collecting his thoughts. "There was a stamp of a dog in red on the alley wall where the boy was last seen."

"That's a new children's gang in Clubb," Lead Constable Norman Pattsz said. A short, thick, balding man with a high-pitched voice, he always seemed looking for someone to challenge him. "My wife's brother told us about them yesterday at dinner. Just a bunch of kids. Petty vandalism, that's all they've done."

"Okay," the Commander said, clearly not impressed by the Lead Constable's input, "Kanhu and Sheinwold, you get this one.

Pull Hanger and Briscola if you need help."

Paix snorted silently. C.K. needed help to get through the day without a drink, and his partner Albert Sheinwold spent most of his day flirting with shop maids and executing men for the Spadros Family.

Then Paix realized what the Commander just said. "Won't there be another search?"

"That's not your concern, Hanger. You've gone above and beyond, but you're needed on your beat. You're welcome to search there. Let the detectives take care of this."

Briscola whispered, "What the fuck?"

Commander Green frowned. "You got something to add, Briscola?"

Briscola straightened. "No, sir."

For Paix, other than the news of a gang battle near the Hedge the night before which had taken every available man to put down, the rest of the briefing went by in a blur.

C.K. was a friend, but the thought of him taking over this case gave Paix the shivers. It was unlikely anything else had been or would be done to find David Bryce.

Paix felt weary. When the briefing was over, Paix went to his desk, opened David's case file flat on the desk. The boy's eyes begged someone to find him.

Paix pocketed the photo.

Someone grabbed his arm. "You listening?"

C.K. had hold of him. The top of a flask stuck out from his jacket pocket. "Commander wants you in his office — now."

Paix hurried up two flights of stairs to the sound of deep raspy coughing and rushed into the Commander's office.

"Close the door." Commander Green sat on the corner of his desk, face red, wiping his mouth with his handkerchief. He panted, "I wanted to talk to you, but you walked off."

"Yes, sir. Sorry, sir."

Briscola stood by the far end of the desk, face pale.

"Son, you're not in trouble," the Commander said. Then he glanced at Briscola. "Either of you." He turned to Paix. "I wasn't happy when the higher-ups kept you here after your little incident last year. But I've been watching you. You're a good cop. It's not easy to be one of those around here."

Paix let out a short laugh in spite of how he felt.

The Commander gestured to Briscola. "Come over here." Once Briscola warily approached, Commander Green said, "I have the feeling you two are going to investigate this no matter what I tell you."

Paix hadn't actually gotten that far yet.

"This whole situation sickens me. Used to be people would put aside their feelings and lend help when there was a child endangered." He shook his head. "Don't tell them I said so, but Barnum and Bailey down there inspire about as much confidence in me as they seem to do to you." He paused for a moment as his breathing slowed. "I don't think I could stand another dead child on my watch."

Paix understood the feeling all too well.

"But the last thing I want is to be surprised by whatever you're up to. So what's your plan?"

Paix shook his head, unwilling to let himself get his hopes up. Could the Commander be asking him to do a Detective's work?

The Commander looked weary. "Come on, Hanger. You've got twenty years on the force. If you were running the game, what would you do?"

"Well —" Paix leaned both hands on the back of a chair to steady himself. "Mrs. Bryce said she was in financial trouble. In Dickens."

The Commander blinked. "You think a bill collector kidnapped the boy?"

"It's not impossible."

"Good gods."

Paix nodded. "I'd do another search, although with the snow it'll be hard to find new evidence."

"Anything else?"

"The traffickers. Spadros is cracking down on them but that doesn't mean they're all gone, just hiding. They might have even moved to other quadrants. We should try to find them and see if they've heard anything."

"Kanhu should be able to help with that."

"And I'd go all the places kids go to see if anyone's seen him."

The Commander walked up to Paix, spoke so only he might hear. "Good. Run everything by Kanhu, let him think it's his idea. But I don't want an uproar during Yuletide. Any reporters come sniffing around, you send them to me."

* * *

Once they were at their desks, Briscola said, "I forgot my nightstick in my room." He lived in the barracks next door. "Be right back."

Paix sat on the corner of his desk waiting for Briscola; C.K. came up to him. "What did Green want?"

"To make sure I helped you." Paix had figured the play he'd make with C.K. on the way down the stairs. "You want me to see what the mother's running from, set up another search, go shake down the traffickers, or go around and ask the local kids if they've seen him?"

C.K. looked pained. "You got way more energy than I do, Hanger." He let out a weary sigh. "Let me set up the background check on the mother. I'll let Sheinwold loose on the traffickers. Those fuckers deserve it." Paix could almost hear the gears grinding in his booze-addled head. "Get Briscola to talk to the kids." He grimaced. "But searching that area again in Yuletide's gonna be a hard sell. They got their beats to run."

"Which you haven't done in two days." When Paix turned around, Lead Constable Pattsz stood scowling, his fists on his hips. "I'm starting to get complaints."

Paix seriously doubted that anyone in his neighborhood complained about not seeing cops around.

"Well," C.K. said. "Looks like you got your assignment." He let out a laugh and walked off towards the exit, going past the background check office without even slowing down.

"Okay, Pattszy," Paix said. The man was his Lead, but almost ten years younger. "I'll get over there."

"You better."

Briscola walked up to them. "Hey, Lead."

Pattsz snapped, "Don't you hey me, young man, you get your lazy fucking no-good ass to work. It's half past eight — neither of you should still be here. And don't even think about showing your faces before nightfall."

Paix picked up a stack of David Bryce's KASLOF fliers on the way out, then he and Briscola hurried to the wagons. Fortunately, one was just coming into the yard. It was embarrassing — not to mention expensive — to have to take a taxi to your beat.

The driver grinned at them. "Miss your wagon, Constables?"

Paix laughed. "Got chewed on by the Commander."

"Hop aboard then, I'll get you going."

On the way, Paix filled Briscola in on what C.K. wanted of them. "Probably best if you take one side and I take another. Kill two birds with a stone."

"I've never seen anyone actually do that," Briscola said.

Paix laughed.

The wagon dropped them off at Beat Station 1, 6th and Snow. They had six blocks down to the Hedge and all the way to the west river to patrol: miles and miles of the most dangerous part of the quadrant save the Pot. By themselves. Each with a wooden nightstick, a pair of handcuffs, and a whistle, against men with guns, knives, and who knew what else.

Sometimes Paix thought they were meant to fail.

He felt grateful he was on day shift, though. Nights were much worse.

The beat sargeant, a round, jolly, blond fellow named Seven Cuebid, did little but sit, read the papers, and eat. He waved, mouth full, as Paix and Briscola signed in. Next to the station was the Messenger stand, with a few of the messengers' little bicycles lying on the ground next to it. An eight year old with bright red hair sat under the awning bench tying his boot.

"Hi," Paix said. "Have you heard of the little boy missing?"

"No, Constable. But I'll pass the word. What's he like?"

Paix gave him a KASLOF flyer.

"Very good, Constable." The boy shoved the flyer in his satchel, hopped on his bicycle, and sped away.

Another boy came from behind the bushes, zipping his pants.

Like David Bryce, the boy was twelve years old with dark hair. Unlike David Bryce, Caddy Arrenegada had blue eyes and looked almost a man: tall, with a bit of yellowish fuzz on his chin. "Need a Messenger today, Constables?"

"We do," Paix said.

"You gonna pay me this time?"

Paix felt irritated at the blatant pitch for a bribe. "You get plenty paid already." Messenger boys who helped billed the department for time spent, which often paid better than they got bringing messages. There were usually several hanging around the booth at the beginning of a shift.

The three started off, Caddy on his bicycle. Paix sent Briscola to the Hedge, while Paix took the north side of 6th Street, planning to meet up at the river for luncheon. They tasked the messenger with posting the KASLOF fliers with David's description.

"Listen out for us, will you?" Briscola said. He sounded nervous at the prospect of patrolling the Hedge alone.

Caddy grinned, shoving the flyers into the back of his waistband. "I will."

Paix strolled along 6th Street, snow crunching under his shoes as he went. The day was cloudy, without a breeze, and his breath puffed white. He waited at Main Road for a break in the traffic going to and from Market Center, then jogged across to continue his patrol.

The narrow street was quiet. The clatter of holiday breakfasts, the smell of Yule logs in the air. A shopkeeper here and there came out to sweep a sidewalk. A hopeful one hung up a sign, but during Yuletide only the grocers ever saw much business.

He crossed Broadway, then continued along 6th towards the river. When he hit the Promenade, he turned towards 5th, to patrol that as well. Their job was to walk the streets and deal with what came to them.

As the day wore on, young men congregated on the corners, children played on the sidewalks, kicked a ball back and forth in the street. No one knew anything. When he spoke to the children, they inevitably ran inside.

After one such time, a man came out with a shotgun. "What you want with my kids?"

Paix turned around to face him. He'd been to this man's home many a time for causing a disturbance; the night shift had been there even more. This guy liked to yell and wave his gun around. He beat his wife on a regular basis, but only once they'd had to take him in, for hitting her with the gun.

No one should hit their woman, Paix thought. The law gave these men too much leniency, that is, when it was even enforced. This man's wife refused to testify, and the prosecutor folded.

Paix said, "A boy's missing."

"I ain't seen no boy when your men came snooping yesterday, and I ain't seen none today." He went in, slamming the door.

Long ago, before all the trouble happened, his partner Jake had griped about the insolent attitude of the people they served.

The Commander overheard. "Don't worry about what they think, Bower. We're cops. Just go out and do your job."

For some reason, that stuck with Paix at moments like this.

By the time he met up with Briscola at 3rd and Promenade, Paix felt ready to go home.

I'm letting myself go weak, he thought, resolving to walk more briskly next time. He gratefully sank into a chair outside the Badugi Bistro — one of many in the city — with his carved wooden bowl of cheap lukewarm noodles and thin sauce. He twirled his wooden fork, took a bite. "Find anything?"

Paix wasn't surprised when Briscola shook his head. When he left, the kid was in such a state he would've been blowing his whistle to pieces if he found so much as a dead cat.

"I checked with the poorhouse," Briscola said. "The Dealers said they'd watch for him."

Paix glanced up, surprised. "Good thinking. Make sure you put that in your report. It'll help you get out of here quicker."

It was Briscola's turn to look surprised.

Paix snorted quietly. "You're young still. You've got a decent chance in the force. I don't know how badly you failed your Entries —"

Briscola flushed red. "I got sick on the test pages."

"— but I've seen lots of you come and go. You're smart. People like you. Being saddled with me isn't a death sentence —"

"I don't think of you like that —"

"— if you're smart about how you do your work. Your report last night was shoddy. Do you use the notebook they gave you?"

Briscola shrugged.

"Use it. There's too much to remember. Look at my report when you get back tonight and compare the two." Paix put his fork in his bowl, his elbows on the table. "Make it your goal to get out of this precinct."

"Why? Seems okay to me."

"The Commander has one foot in the grave. Everyone else is either incompetent, drunk, on Party Time, or wanting to fight someone. You stay here too long, you'll be marked as one of them."

"What about you?"

And then there's me. Paix grinned to himself, stirring bits of noodle in the pool of sauce at the bottom of his bowl. "I just can't seem to mind my own business."

4

They returned their dishes to the collection area and set off again, each to their own patrol, Paix taking the Hedge this time.

A clean, wide alley ran behind the shops along the Promenade, a neatly clipped privet hedge ten foot thick and tall past that. The hundred-foot wide graveled area with tracks for the trains going to and from the island ran along behind that, then the Hedge loomed. Yew and holly bushes forty feet wide stood along the tracks, with the black wrought-iron of the Fence bound up in their thorny leaves.

The Travelers' Board had its own men just to patrol the tracks. Paix had heard rumors that trespassers were buried there, but no one had ever confirmed it, and he'd never dared investigate.

A low-rent shop or two always tried to take hold past the train tracks on 1st Boulevard, but only curious tourists ever came this far. For these hapless shops, the turnover was high, and today they stood empty. Past them, the row of ancient boarded-up homes and businesses stretched as far as he could see.

For the first few blocks, the boulevard was clean, with attractive plantings down the center which could withstand any climate. As they walked out of view of the Promenade, however, cracks appeared in the sidewalk. Gaps in the inch-thick wrought iron made during the Coup had never been repaired; if you knew where to look, you could push past the thorns and cross through. A few ragged children had done just that, disappearing back through when they saw Paix approach.

The bushes grew eight feet in from the Fence in places, well deep enough on this side to hide a small body. Paix used his nightstick to peer around in the branches, finding a great deal of trash and a dead possum but nothing else.

Near the Main Road, the street was better maintained, and the plantings reappeared. Paix crossed over once traffic allowed to finish the last block between Main and Snow. That done, he peered across the street. Empty broken windows gaped at him.

Sometimes quadrant-folk too proud to move to the Pot stayed in the abandoned buildings for a while. Paix usually let them live in peace, but occasionally the Commander would order him to roust whoever was there.

Once in a while, a gang of Acey-Deuceys — the most violent of the young Spadros men — would be sent to clear them out. Paix suspected that was what caused the commotion the night before: there seemed a great deal more destruction today.

The buildings were empty. On the third house from Broadway, Paix found the body of an old man under a table, an empty bottle of cheap liquor beside him. The man had not so much as a penny in his pockets, nor any identification. No sign of struggle; it was as if the fellow fell asleep and never woke. Going to the front porch, Paix blew his whistle: one long burst, then four short bursts, waited a second, then four bursts, then waited, then four again.

The Spadros Family had assigned a messenger to each street: a blond boy, perhaps ten, waved as he whizzed past on his bicycle to fetch the coroner's wagon.

Paix noted the time and details in his notebook, then unfolded a foot square red cloth from his inner jacket pocket, tying it to a dead bush in front to mark the house. Then he continued to search the other homes until he heard the coroner's whistle a half-hour later. Paix jogged the three blocks to the coroner's men, who peered at the house but seemed unwilling to step inside. One held a clipboard, making notes of his own.

"In here," Paix panted. He retrieved his red flag, folded it, then led them to the body.

The men nodded, pulling on masks and gloves, and Paix went back outside to escape the inevitable smell. The two men came out carrying the body in a sheet.

"Looked natural to me," Paix said; they nodded. The back of the truck held three bodies already, and a stack of sheets. He waved to them as they left, jogging back to where he'd left off.

A few houses down, a trash can lay on its side in a muddy puddle of melting snow. David's KASLOF flyers had been flung into it.

Paix kicked the can; the sodden clump of flyers didn't move. "That little wretch!" He leaned against the wall, discouraged.

A boy's laughter. Caddy stood there with his bicycle. "Maybe next time, you pay me," he said, then rode off.

Paix ran to the street. "You bottom-dealing check-chopper!" He heaved a brick at the boy, which missed, shattering on the ground beside Caddy's back wheel the boy as raced away.

What was he going to do?

He walked the mile back to the beat sergeant's booth. Sergeant Constable Cuebid had his feet up on his desk reading the sporting column.

"Caddy Arrenegada threw my KASLOF flyers in the mud," Paix said.

"Whaddya want me to do about it?"

"I don't want him around here anymore."

"I can't stop him coming round."

"Fine help you are." Paix stalked off to finish his patrol.

Paix walked 3rd Street, then finished searching the houses on 1st. By the time he got to 2nd, Bryce Fabrics was closed, and Paix felt reluctant to knock, seeing as he had no real news.

But perhaps David Bryce had returned home. So Paix knocked. No one answered. So he returned to Briscola and the wagons, and headed to the station.

* * *

Paix went to the desk to hand over his reports for the day. "If Caddy Arrenegada puts in a bill for serving me or my partner, deny it."

I should arrest him for obstruction, Paix thought. If he could catch him. They really needed their own wagons, like the guys in the better areas had.

The desk clerk blinked. "What'd he do?"

"Threw my KASLOF flyers in the mud. The ones for the

34

missing kid. Whole stack ruined."

"Insolent little fucker," the clerk said. "I hate when he and his brothers come here. I'll pass it along, but don't get your hopes up."

"What do you mean?"

"His dad just made Associate."

"Shit," Paix said. Associates weren't sworn in yet, but the Family still protected them and their own. No wonder the kid was so cheeky: he probably thought he could get away with anything.

He was probably right.

The background check office had no record of C.K. putting in a request, so Paix put one in for him. "He likely forgot."

The clerk, perhaps nineteen, snickered.

C.K. might be a lazy drunk, but he was a friend. "Don't you dare mock a Detective Senior Constable in this department."

The man went pale. "My apologies, Constable."

"And I want this on my desk when I return from Krissmiss."

It was early yet, so instead of going home, Paix went to the far side of Market Center, the legal district, and knocked on a door.

Jake Bower opened it, his dark brown face immediately going from his usual cheer to a bristling scowl filled with disdain. "What do you want?"

Jake's reaction hurt Paix more than if the man would have hit him. "I want you to leave Reina alone."

"What have you done to her? She looks terrible."

"You have to stop! She's afraid to answer the door." Which Paix didn't know was true, just something he felt.

Jake flinched; Paix immediately regretted saying anything.

Jake shook his head, stricken. "She's afraid of me? Why? I've never even raised a hand to her —"

"I know." This had gotten out of hand. "I'm sorry. I should never have said that."

They fell silent, and Paix felt that somehow this time out of all the times he'd come here was different. Neither Jake nor Reina had ever given him a straight answer as to what happened between them. "Why'd she leave you? What really happened?"

Jake let out a breath, turned away, his hand on his forehead.

"So many things. That's all I can get out of her, 'So many things'." His hand dropped to his side. "I have to know why my daughter died. And ... well, when ... you know —"

Paix nodded. The brawl outside the briefing room, when they'd mutually decided to kill each other. Everyone said Jake started it, which after the business with Peedro Sluff was why he was let go. But when Jake called Reina a whore ....

Jake turned to put his hand up on the door post, and it seemed to Paix that the old gears fell into place. "You know, we used to be friends. First you back Sluff —"

Were they really going to have this conversation again? "No. I **never** backed him —"

"— then while we're still grieving, you — you take my wife! By the Dealer, Paix —"

This surprised him. Jake never called him that unless he was truly busted. When Jake's mother died. When his daughter disappeared.

When they found her body.

"— please, stop and think about what you're doing. How can you live with yourself?"

But I love her. And she loves me.

At least Jake hadn't hit him yet. "Look, I know this hurts —"

Jake bristled, his hand dropping to his side. "You're damn right it does!"

"You've gone through a hell of a lot. I understand that. I never wanted to hurt you. I don't want to now. But you gotta face reality. It's been over a year." Paix tried a different tack, hoping to get his former partner to see reason. "I'm not forcing her to stay with me. She doesn't want to go back. Please, for everyone's sake. Let her go."

"Why? You want me to drag her name through the mud, and for what? So you can get an heir?"

She's suffering right now because of you. At that thought, he saw what he needed to do. "Don't come to my home again."

"Or what?"

Did Jake have a gun? "I don't want trouble, but there will be if you keep harassing her." Jake should know Paix wouldn't send the police after him ... but it was a temptation.

"I can't see my own wife, is that it?"

"Not if she doesn't want to see you." Suddenly, the day crashed in on him. He felt exhausted. "The game's over, Jake. There **is** no play here that will let you win. Please. For your own sake. Let her go." He turned and left, his back crawling, his heart pounding.

But he never looked back.

* * *

Paix couldn't spare the penny for a taxi-carriage, no matter how much his feet hurt. As he walked home, Paix thought about little David Bryce. He couldn't keep the boy's eyes out of his mind.

Could he and Reina have a child someday? It seemed impossible.

This last time she'd gotten pregnant had been the worst so far. If only they had the money for Reina to take the daily tea, rather than this larger dose.

Thank the gods for that apothecary, whoever she was. If not for her, Reina would be in the Pot by now.

Paix used to believe women should be sent to the Pot for the temerity to bear a child outside the marriage bed. He didn't know what to believe anymore.

More than anything, he wanted a child of his own. Not only to have an heir, as Jake seemed to think. Paix just wanted a son.

I'd treat him right. I'd raise him to be a good man. I'd let him do whatever good work he wanted to do, not cast him aside — at that thought, he felt bitter — like my father did to me.

A man walked ahead, a child holding each hand. One looked up, and the pride on the boy's face stopped Paix in his tracks.

I want this.

"Are you well, Constable?"

An woman peered back at Paix, dressed in widow's brown, and he was reminded of the boy's mother. "I'm well, madam."

She nodded and moved on.

Am I well?

He didn't actually know.

When Paix got home, the aroma of roasted meat made his stomach growl. Reina came to kiss him with a smile.

"I'm so glad to be home to you," Paix said.

She pulled him close without a word.

She understands me, he thought. *How am I so fortunate?*

He changed his clothes, washed his face and hands, sat in front of his meal. One of the ways Reina seemed to understand was that she rarely pressed him about his work or troubles. She knew he would tell her when he was ready.

"This is good," he said.

She blushed, and put down her fork, taking his hand across the table.

His heart felt full. "I'll take care of you, Reina, no matter what. You have my word."

"I know."

"I'll go to the Pot myself before I let you be sent there."

She peered at their hands for a moment. "You talked to Jake."

Paix nodded.

"How is he?"

Paix stared at his plate, shook his head.

Her shoulders slumped. "Even if I went back —"

Chill fingers squeezed his heart. "Don't even consider it —"

"But even if I did, he wouldn't be happy. He's consumed with grief. He wears a smile, even seems happy. But underneath he's filled with bitterness and envy. He wants me in his house. But he doesn't want **me**."

Surprised, Paix said, "Why do you think so?"

"If he did, he wouldn't have spent his whole time over the past three years chasing his paranoia. He doesn't even consider she was my child too!" She took a deep breath, let it out. "You were there for us both. Do you regret," she raised their hands a bit, then let them fall, "this?"

Paix leaned forward. "Never. Not for one second." He leaned back, glanced away. "I do regret causing him pain. That I regret deeply." He peered in her eyes, intertwined his fingers in hers. "But I bless every moment I have with you. Never doubt that."

* * *

It always seemed odd, having Krissmass Day off, so close to Yuletide Center.

Paix had asked his Constable about it back when he was a Trainee. No one knew what the day meant, other than a day for extra gift-giving. No one knew why the people who had to work during Yuletide — police, fire, doctors — didn't work on that day. Or why the ones who did — apprentices, new hires — were always paid double.

"A holy tradition from before the Catastrophe," one very old man had told Paix when he was a boy. "My grandfather said his grandfather told him his grandfather told **him** that in the far-distant past, there were specially-made Cards that the Shuffler dealt just for those born at Krissmiss." The old man had said it with awe in his voice.

Paix never learned the truth of the matter. And none of it made sense. Where were these Holy Cards today? Were those so born all evildoers, their Cards burnt in the Fire? Could the Inerrant Shuffler have possibly lost the whole lot?

It sounded like blasphemy.

But whatever the reality, he felt grateful for a day to rest with the woman he loved.

She'd tied green and gold ribbons around the house, placed pine boughs around the edges of the floor. He kissed her sleeping forehead, considering what she'd said the night before. Did she regret leaving her husband? Did she sit here alone, weeping over her dead daughter?

"You ask too many questions," his father once told him.

Paix smiled to himself. *Enjoy your fucking day off, you fool. Stop asking why.*

The only reason he was here was that the Commander wasn't allowed to give him holiday duty: as a Constable, his pay was much higher. Otherwise, he'd be out there in the cold patrolling like whatever donkeys the Commander had put on assignment.

He remembered the pittance he'd received back when he was a Probationary, trying to sleep in the barracks amidst snoring men. He could have stayed here, but back then, he just wanted to fit in.

I would not want to go back to those days.

Reina turned over in her sleep. Paix got up to light candles and make tea. He wanted her to wake up to something beautiful.

5

When Paix returned to work the next day, to his surprise the background report was actually on his desk. Not a lot there, but what was there made him sit down.

Inquiries had been made about Mrs. Bryce from outside the dome. One was from a Constable Highcard of the Central Dickens Police Department as to her whereabouts. The other was from a legal firm representing Mr. Deuce Kiga, a bill collector of Dickens who was trying to have her and her children extradited for non-payment and flight.

Both inquiries were denied.

Paix wasn't sure why anyone would even bother. Bridges — or more to the point, the Clubb crime syndicate, which controlled the means to communicate with the other domes — never extradited anyone, not even murderers. Certainly not a widow woman who owed some bill collector.

Had either of these men entered the city? He went to the desk. "Is Detective Senior Constable Kanhu here?"

"Haven't seen him."

He hadn't been at the pre-shift briefing either. Too much Krissmiss merriment? Paix resolved to stop by C.K.'s house on the way home. "Thanks."

Paix went up the stairs to his Lead Constable's desk.

Lead Constable Norman Pattsz sat paring his nails with a letter opener. He glanced up. "What do you want?"

Paix gave him a summary of the situation. "What's the best way to learn if these men tried to get in the city? Right now they're our primary suspects for the boy's kidnapping."

"You're sure it's a kidnapping?"

Paix almost asked if he could sit down but decided against it.

Pattszy was all about protocol. "The boy just moved here from Dickens a few weeks ago. The family has no friends. No one has seen the boy. I suppose he could be dead, but I believe he was lured away. This man Kiga has ample motive; this Constable may be working for him."

Pattsz nodded, his face serious. "I see your point. I'll put in a request to have these men stopped if they appear at the zeppelin station. Then we can question them."

Which could take weeks to go through "proper channels". "They may have the boy now."

Pattsz frowned. "I'm not going to break procedure because you feel anxious. Go about your duties, and let me take care of mine." He returned to paring his nails.

And that was the end of that. Paix collected Briscola — who was more than a bit hung over — and started his day.

The first place they went was Bryce Fabrics. When they entered the shop, Paix said, "Madam —"

Mrs. Bryce said, "Enough! It's bad enough you people come here day after day asking for money, but unless you've found my son, I want you to leave!"

Paix stood there, mouth open. "Who's been here?"

She batted her handkerchief at them. "Some detective. Now get out!" She pushed them out, slamming the door behind them.

Paix and Briscola stood there on the cracked sidewalk.

"But we weren't asking for money," Briscola said. "Do you think Detective Senior Constable Kanhu was here?"

"No," Paix said, "but I think I know who was."

They found Detective Constable Sheinwold sitting at the bar over at the Backdoor Saloon. Howell and his friends sat at the same table they did the last time. "Watch yourself," Paix told Briscola. "This could get ugly."

Paix leaned on one elbow next to Sheinwold. "Got a minute, Detective?"

Briscola took up position on the other side of Albert Sheinwold, a deeply tanned, prematurely graying man in his early forties who looked well drunk already. It wasn't noon yet.

Sheinwold's pale blue eyes were bloodshot. "Sure, I'd love to talk with ya. Siddown."

Neither one of them sat.

Paix said, "Why are you bothering that widow woman for money? Spadros doesn't pay you enough?"

The men sitting at the table close by laughed. Sheinwold's face flushed red. "Shut up, Hanger, you fouled-hand nit."

"Now she won't talk to us. I told C.K. I'd help him, but I can't do much if you keep harassing her."

Sheinwold grabbed Paix by the collar, and a click came from behind.

Howell had a revolver pointed at Sheinwold's head. "Not in my bar, copper. And not him. He may be a cop, but he s my cop. Understand?"

Paix felt confused. Did Howell think he could use him for something later on?

Sheinwold laughed, but tension lay thick in the air. "And here I thought you were nothing but a misdeal." He got up from the barstool as Howell retreated, then came very close, his voice pitched so no one else might hear, pointing a finger. "You fuck with me in front of people again and you're dead." He stalked out.

Paix went over to Howell and said quietly, "Let's get one thing straight. I'm not for sale."

Howell said just as quietly, "You want me to have my boys here call him back so he can kill you?"

Paix didn't have anything to say to this.

"Then you're gonna be more grateful when I go out of my way to help."

"I am."

"Listen, Hanger," he said, raising his voice to a normal tone. "We were boys together. You might say we started off in the same spot," he gestured off to the side with the gun in his hand, "then took different paths. But you and me, we got one thing in common — we care about making sure people get taken care of."

Paix thought about it a moment to see if he agreed with this, then nodded.

"I help you, you help me, everyone gets taken care of. Right?" He glanced at Briscola, who looked quite pale, then back. "Like that little deal we made the other day."

If I use the word "informant," he dies, Paix thought. That's the one thing the Family can't stand for. "A business arrangement."

"Yes, indeed," Howell said. Then he holstered his gun and his tone turned quiet, serious. "I can't find anyone who's heard of the kid. But I'll keep asking."

"Thanks, Eighty," Paix said in a normal tone. "Good seeing you again."

Outside, Briscola said, "Did you know he was gonna help?"

"Sometimes you gotta just bet," Paix said, "and hope you have the cards behind you."

* * *

Paix and Briscola walked the rest of their beat together, just in case Sheinwold got it in his mean drunken head to come after them. But they didn't see him the rest of the day.

The day after Krissmiss was usually quiet. A dead man fished out of the river, a lost dog, a domestic dispute. All in a day's work.

After Paix got his reports done — leaving out the incident in the bar — he walked up to C.K.'s place near 48th and Snow.

The houses this far up had little lawns, bushes, even some fruit trees. C.K.'s lawn hadn't been cut in months, and the bushes were overgrown. His wife answered the door in a house dress which seemed to be on backwards. Her words slurred as she spoke, and she smelled of alcohol. "Was wondering when one of you would come by." She leered at him. "I remember you. You gonna steal me away too?"

Hardly. "How's he doing?"

"Oh, he'll be fine. Wanna come in?"

"If he's awake."

She turned into the house. "Cartas! You got company." Then she turned to Paix. "He'll get up. You want anything?"

"No, thank you." From the condition of the house, he was almost afraid to see their cups and dishes.

Paix remembered what an alive, active man C.K. was when he joined the force, eyes full of hope. This broken, shambling creature was a different being altogether.

C.K. peered around, eyes bleary, unshaven, then collapsed into an overstuffed chair. "Sit down. You're making me tired just watching you."

Paix sat on the sofa. "You look terrible."

C.K. chuckled. "I've felt better."

"Didn't see you today. Just wondering how we could help."

"We? I don't see your pup. Leave him outside?"

Paix allowed himself a slight smile. Briscola **was** young. So was C.K., long ago. "We need to talk."

"Aw, hell. What's gone wrong now?"

"Sheinwold's been shaking the widow down for money. The woman can barely pay her fees."

A long string of slurred profanity followed.

"I talked to him already," Paix said, "but I thought you should know. Went to see her today and she threw us out."

"I'll tell him to leave her alone. I'll go talk to her myself." He peered up at Paix. "Anything I can tell her?"

Paix shrugged. "We have a couple of leads, but —"

"Nothing to get her hopes up about." C.K. leaned forward, elbows on his knees, hands together. "Hell of a Yuletide."

Paix nodded.

"You remember when we used to dream about making a difference? Bring some respect to the force?" C.K. seemed to collapse into himself a little. "What happened to us?"

Paix thought this was probably not something he wanted to answer honestly. C.K. had started taking a penny here and there to overlook some minor misdeed. Now he stood guard for Party Time shipments and was paid in cheap booze. "Don't know."

"I do," C.K. said. "It got easy to do what everyone else did."

Paix wanted to be different. "What do you need?" Then he laughed. "As long as it doesn't cost anything."

C.K. laughed. "Indeed." He leaned back, closed his eyes. "The stamp on the wall. I looked into it. That Clubb quadrant street gang — Red Dog, Red Dogs, something like that. They've been recruiting children in Spadros his age." He opened his eyes. "Maybe the kid refused to go with them and it got ugly."

6

On the next day's trip over the bridge into Spadros, Paix sat in the wagon beside the chattering trainees quartered on the island.

Something had been bothering him for a while now.

People were smuggled into Bridges, not out. Financial refugees from Dickens, criminals fleeing an Azimoff death mark, indentured servants from Nitivali. But in. Not out.

Whores who didn't like Bridges might sell themselves to a recruiter from Chicago, but as they said, that was business. And the Romani didn't trade in children — in fact, trying to sell them one might be more likely to end with your throat cut.

This was Yuletide, the busiest travel time of the year, and passenger flights both ways had been booked for months. The chance of this Deuce Kiga or one of his bounty hunters getting into Bridges during the three weeks since the Bryce family left Dickens was slim, even if he hadn't attracted the attention of the Clubbs with his extradition request. The chance of the man getting to the Bryce's home and out of the city with a uncooperative child in that time was almost zero.

David Bryce wouldn't have run away: with his father newly dead, staying close to his mother and brother would be his top priority. Plus, where would he go?

That left kidnapping: not for ransom — the family obviously had none to give — but for enslavement or murder.

Four days the boy had been missing. Paix had a bad feeling about this.

He turned to the Trainees, barely more than boys themselves, really. "You know a gang called Red Dog?"

"Yeah," one said, a gangly red-haired youth with a lisp and a wall-eye. "Bunch of kids." He scoffed. "They tried to get my little brother to join but he's the Spadros street messenger for east 23rd." The Trainee spoke with pride. "He's smart, good-looking, moving up in the world. Got no time for such rubbish."

Paix flinched internally at the name but kept his face still. *So they got to you already.* "Where do they loiter?"

"In Spadros? Around 20th, east side."

East side. Bryce Fabrics wasn't even in their area. He got out as the wagon stopped at the station. "Thanks."

C.K. wasn't at pre-shift briefing.

Sheinwold stood by the wall, glowering at him.

When a pause came, Paix said, "Update on David Bryce. Detective Senior Constable Kanhu sends his regards," Paix let his eyes flicker to Sheinwold, "and wants us to check on this for him." He pulled out the drawing of the stamp and passed it around. "Group calling themselves the Red Dogs. Anything you know of their activities in **Spadros** quadrant —"

At this, Pattsz bristled.

"— would help."

The trainees gave Paix a startled glance, as if surprised that anything they'd said could be of use. The Constables on the upper east beats knew the mark. "Bunch of children," one said. "Eight to maybe fifteen years old. They run in twos, like to throw rocks at shop windows. Want us to round up some?"

"Sure," Paix said. "Ask about the boy, but don't scare them. They're possible witnesses, not suspects." If they were that far out of their area and saw David taken, even the few who'd speak with the police might be too afraid to talk if someone got aggressive with them.

The Commander hadn't missed the finer points of the exchange. "Sheinwold? This is your case. You got something to add?" The implication hung in the air: *or are you slacking off?*

Sheinwold shifted to his other foot, still leaning against the wall. "Widow's got nothing."

"Left," Briscola whispered, too loudly.

Those around them snickered.

Paix froze.

Sheinwold's eyes narrowed. "Talked to all the local traffickers.

No one's heard anything."

Commander Green said, "I want you to go to every brothel in the Pot and find out if they've seen the kid. Look at me, Sheinwold. I want this done quietly. You got that? If I hear about anyone beaten up or you manhandling my Constables again —"

Paix and Sheinwold exchanged a glance: Paix was astonished, Sheinwold, furious.

"— there's gonna be trouble."

Green must have gotten word through the Backdoor.

If Sheinwold were a tea kettle, steam would be pouring from his ears. But he mumbled, "Yes, Commander."

"All right, everyone, let's go — stay safe out there."

After glaring at Paix, Sheinwold stormed out.

Paix turned to Briscola. "What the hell was that?"

Briscola said, "What?"

"What did I tell you about keeping your mouth shut? I don't care how funny you think you are, you don't do that in pre-shift briefing." Paix lowered his voice to a whisper. "I don't want to be called to the scene of your homicide. Do you understand?"

Briscola paled. "Yeah. I understand."

Paix nodded to the Commander, who leaned against the desk watching them. "Come on," Paix said to Briscola, "let's go."

They visited the whole area again — the grocery stores, the bars, showed David's picture to the kids playing by the Hedge. No one had seen him, even before he disappeared.

Paix ran into the Family man, starting his rounds to pick up the Spadros Family's monthly fees. "That the new family? Seen the mother out a time or two, but never the little one. Older one's been round asking for work but —" The man grimaced in disgust. "— we don't deal with outsiders. 'Sides, he's dressed too good for any job down here. Told him he should go up to 40th and check the shops there."

Hell of a walk for a young man grieving his father. "Thanks."

"Let me pay their fees this month," Briscola said, digging out two pennies for the man.

The man took a narrow envelope from his pocket and dropped them in. Then he added the name to a list on its front and folded it shut. "I'm sure she'll be much obliged." He turned to knock on the door.

Paix smiled to himself as they walked away. He'd started out doing the same thing. "Don't make that a habit."

Briscola glanced at him, surprised. "Why?"

"They'll thank you the first time, and maybe even the second — but when you stop, they'll hate you for it. Blame you when they can't make their fees." He'd learned that lesson the hard way.

"Okay." Briscola stared at his feet, kicked a rock. "I just wanted to help out. Seeing all that's happened."

"I know."

The day, overall, was a quiet one, which suited Paix just fine. Home with his beautiful Reina over the weekend, then two days on, then New Year's Eve.

Paix was looking forward to New Year's Eve. Their tradition was to go to the Plaza, have a picnic dinner on the lawn, and watch the fireworks until midnight. Then he was off for New Year's Day.

It didn't get any better than this.

* * *

When Paix came in on Monday, the night desk clerk was putting on his jacket to leave, but had a note for him. "A Mrs. Bryce came by yesterday about her son's case. I told her I'd give Detective Senior Constable Kanhu the message, but I know you've been helping out."

Paix leaned forward. "Did they find him?"

"No, and I really couldn't talk to her much. Why do people try to kill each other on the holidays?"

Paix chuckled. "I dunno."

Sheinwold came in sporting a black eye, but was able to report he'd been to all the brothels in Spadros. "They haven't seen him. And I didn't see him either."

"Good job, Detective Constable," the Commander said. "And welcome back, Kanhu."

C.K. looked as if he'd eaten something disagreeable.

After the briefing — which other than the list of cases piled on the detectives, was fairly short — Paix handed C.K. the note about Mrs. Bryce. "You want me to go over?"

"Naw," C.K. said, rubbing his bruised right hand with his left. "I'll handle it."

Paix gestured in Sheinwold's direction with his chin. "What happened there?"

"Not your problem, Hanger."

Paix realized then that the two had words. Fists, too, by the look of C.K.'s hand. "You give that to him?"

"Why don't you mind your own business?" C.K. was joking, but there was an edge to it.

Briscola had stood aside waiting for Paix to catch up. "What's wrong with him?"

Paix said, "His hand hurts."

Briscola glanced at the two detectives and started laughing.

* * *

Paix and Briscola got into the wagon along with the others, and he watched as the men were dropped at their beat stations along Snow Street.

When they got to Beat Station 1, they signed in, Paix first, then Briscola, the two Constables from east beat waiting their turn. Sergeant Constable Cuebid didn't greet them.

Paix said, "You well, Cue?"

He glanced at them, then away. "Yeah, sure."

Something didn't feel right. "Come on," Paix told Briscola, "let's go." They went round the corner of the station.

Six young men were there.

They had bricks.

Caddy said, "Detective Constable Sheinwold says hello."

7

Pain.

A white room with white curtains and white sheets.

Paix felt exhausted. His head hurt the most out of everything, and he tasted blood.

I should never have thrown that brick.

A woman dressed in pale green with a pale green scarf of the same material completely covering her hair came in. "Oh, good, you're awake. I'll let them know." She left without another word.

A bit old to be a Dealers' Apprentice, Paix thought.

Reina rushed over and knelt, pressing his hand to her cheek. It only hurt a little. What really hurt were the tears in her eyes. "Oh, Paix," she whispered.

He smiled at her. "Hi."

The Commander walked in.

Paix said to him, "Did they find the boy?"

He shook his head.

"Paix," Reina said urgently. "They arrested Jake."

Paix frowned at her. "Why?"

"How are you, son?" The Commander came over to the other side of the bed. "I brought you the paper."

"Jake didn't do it," Paix said. "He wouldn't do this. It was Sheinwold."

Reina let out a gasp.

Commander Green's eyebrows rose. "Are you sure?"

"Caddy Arrenegada and five others held the bricks." He winced at a sudden pain in his side. "But they said Sheinwold sent them." He thought about how Cuebid was acting. "Cuebid knew it was coming." He looked between them, which hurt a lot. "How's Briscola?"

"Badly sprained arm, broken nose, bashed about — gonna be down for a week." The Commander seemed angry. "Sheinwold's denying anything to do with it." He paced a bit more, then faced him. "East beat chased Caddy and his boys a half mile. But they got away — they've dropped out of sight." He began to pace, then scowled. "Sheinwold, huh? I'm gonna nail that fucker to the wall. Officers attacking each other, using little thugs instead of taking care of their own problems — what's this city coming to?"

Tears ran down Reina's cheeks.

Commander Green glanced at her. "Don't worry, my dear — I'll have them let Jake loose." He walked out.

Paix felt sick, confused. "Why'd they arrest Jake?"

"He has cause to hurt you," she said. "And he's not protected anymore."

Not that being in the force, or even being Howell's friend seemed to be protecting him much these days. "What day is it?" All he remembered was a drugged haze of pain for what seemed like forever.

"The first. New Year's Day." Her shoulders slumped. "You missed the fireworks."

Paix raised a bruised and scraped hand to stroke the side of her face. "They'll be there next year." Then he had a thought. "If I don't have to work during the Celebration, there's sure to be fireworks then."

She smiled at him. "We won't even have to pay for a taxi." They lived a few blocks from the train station, close enough to walk there.

Paix peered at the newspaper. On the front, the portraits of the Four Families: beautiful, well-fed women and hard-faced men. He remembered how empty Mrs. Bryce's home was. *They feasted last night, while their people struggle to survive.* He shook his head and put the paper away. A soft knock beyond the curtains, to his right. "Come in."

Briscola was wheeled in by a different Dealers' Apprentice, young and pretty. His left eye was blackened, his nose was bandaged, he had scrapes all over his face, and his right arm was in a sling. "Damn," Briscola said, "you look even worse than I do."

Paix chuckled, then winced at a sudden pain in his side. "They letting you go?"

"My brother's coming to get me. Thought I'd check on you."

"Glad it wasn't a homicide."

Briscola snorted. "Me too. Once we get better, let's say we get some guys together and —"

"No," Paix said. "Fold that in now." He peered into Briscola's eyes. "You don't hurt other cops, Leone. Ever. You hear me? Sheinwold went way off the table, and it's going to cost him his shield, his pension, everything. He'll stay out of the Prison because he's a Spadros horse —"

Reina sighed, and Paix realized he was talking more than he should. "— but he's finished." The thought made him sad. He remembered when Sheinwold joined the force — a bright, likable man. "Don't end up like him."

Briscola stared at the bedsheets and nodded slowly.

"I know it's hard," Paix said. "We got a bad break, but we survived. Just take it one round at a time."

* * *

They sent Paix home two days later with orders not to exert himself in any way for a week. So it was the next Monday before he was back on the job.

Because the gang who'd ambushed them hadn't yet been caught, Briscola had been on desk duty for his own safety until Paix returned. Several pairs of weekend duty men from various precincts had been patrolling their beat for them.

But there was one piece of good news. A young man, perhaps fifteen, had been seen laying down cards with the Red Dog stamp on them over on the lower east side, and a KASLOF had been printed with his description. While the weekend crew hadn't located the kid, the east side beat cops assured Paix and C.K. they'd find him soon.

As usual after the holidays, lots of bodies had been found. A whole crew — the Wharf Patrol — were tasked just with collecting the bodies from the shorelines in the middle of the night before the public appeared at the waterfront.

Turned out that after a week's suspension, that was where Sheinwold had been sent. After the briefing, Commander Green told Paix and Briscola himself. "This goes way above my rank," he said. "Chief of Police level."

Paix had a brief enraged flash of how good it would feel to beat Sheinwold's smug face bloody. "I don't believe this! Fucking Spadros Family." He shook his head, rage turning to disgust. "This is their doing. I was out more than a week after almost being killed, and he doesn't even get that much suspension? So if they would've killed me, what then? Doesn't the department care about us at all?"

Commander Green stood watching. "Dismissed."

He already said there was nothing he could do, Paix thought. *It's not his fault.*

For an instant, he felt compassion for this ailing old man trying to make sense out of it all. "Hell," Paix said. "I don't know why I'm surprised. I should've expected it. Thanks for letting me know." He turned and walked away, mumbling, "Guess I should be glad I've lived as long as I have."

Briscola ran up beside him. "What do we do?"

"We watch our backs," Paix said bitterly. "No one else will."

While Wharf Patrol was where all the worst offenders of the force were to report at night, Sheinwold was loose during the day. What would he do next?

C.K. still hadn't found David Bryce. But he had a stack of homicides, and he hadn't been assigned a new partner yet. It seemed unless they found a body, David would be just another picture on the missing board.

When Paix and Briscola — who still had his arm in a sling — arrived at the beat station, a stocky, dark-skinned sergeant sat there. "Sergeant Constable Cuebid was transferred," the man said. "Don't know where." His lip curled in disdain. "Not sure I care."

Paix chuckled. Cuebid was good for eating and reading the paper, and that was about it. "You run across a kid named Caddy Arrenegada —"

"Arrest him." He said this as if he'd been told that a dozen times today already. He opened a drawer, pulling out a KASLOF flyer. "Got a portrait of him here."

"He's the one that did this to us," Briscola said. "Him and his friends."

The man peered at the page and raised an eyebrow. "He's twelve?" He made his hand into a gun shape, then made a firing motion. "Better to put that kind down."

Paix felt uncomfortable with this sort of talk. "I don't kill children, Sergeant Constable. Good day."

He and Briscola slowly walked their beat together, and several people came out to say hello. "I didn't like those other men they sent," one old woman said. "You feeling better?"

That was nice for once, he thought. "I am," Paix replied, although he still felt and looked like hell. "Thank you."

"Guess they don't appreciate you until you're not there." Briscola gingerly rubbed the skin beside his nose. "Maybe they'll be more grateful."

"For a while, anyway," Paix said.

That first day of patrol after being in bed almost two weeks left Paix exhausted — he went straight home and to sleep. He woke in the middle of the night, disoriented, then left Reina sleeping to eat his dinner, which she'd kept warm in the oven.

How could he keep working like this? Paix remembered how proud he used to be of his work. Now, it seemed as if there weren't any rules any more.

I just want to do my job.

Come home to Reina.

Get that boy back to his mother.

Paix refused to believe David Bryce was dead.

Somehow I'd know, he thought, which surprised him. But it was true — he just didn't know how he knew.

"Paix?" Reina was sitting up in bed. "Are you well?"

He smiled at her. "Just hungry. Sorry to wake you."

She got up, drew her robe around herself, and padded over to kiss his forehead, sit beside him. She put her arm around his shoulders, rubbed his upper back. "I'm glad I did. I have something to tell you."

She sounded excited, and this drew his curiosity. "What?"

"I went out yesterday, and —"

Sheinwold and those kids were still out there. The one way they could really hurt him was by hurting her. "**What!?**"

"My champion," Reina said fondly. She put her hand on his. "I've been an officer's wife for many years. I know how to protect myself. Besides, I never left the island."

He sighed with relief. "Go on."

"I went to your cousin's booth on the Plaza."

Paix nodded. Lane Tableau and her husband Heap ran a booth selling knitted items. "Are they still Bridgers?"

Reina nodded. "They'd sell more if they'd quit shoving flyers and pamphlets at their customers." She chuckled. "Do you remember how I used to spin?"

Paix nodded. Reina was good at it, too. Then his eye went to the spinning wheel in the corner, only half seen when he stumbled in the night before. "You're going to spin for them!"

She beamed. "You are truly brilliant. They know someone who sells wool wholesale. I got my wheel, and —"

"Did Jake bother you?"

She smiled slyly. "I still have a key."

Paix laughed aloud. "Good for you."

"— and they'll let me sit with them. It benefits us all — I can take commissions, they have someone to help watch the booth, and I can get more air and sun. The apothecary said that would help my recovery."

Paix took her face in his hands and kissed it. "And you'll be in plain view of the station." *She'll be safe.* He hugged her tightly, eyes stinging. "I'm so proud of you."

"This is for us both. I'll be a Plaza member," she whispered. She pulled back to peer in his eyes. "You know what that means?"

He shook his head.

"I can get vegetable leftovers, ends and bones the butchers can't sell. I can get deals from the other vendors. And one day I might even be able to get a booth of my own. Don't you see? When you retire, we might become owners!"

Owners. The thought took Paix aback. Have a business of their own? "You've done very well!"

"You work so hard for us. I can't sit here idly any more whilst you risk your life." She touched the side of his face. "We can get through this, my love. You'll see."

57

8

Early the next morning, Paix carried Reina's wheel to his cousins' booth. Heap Tableau, a dumpy pale man with thinning mousy brown hair, merely glanced up at them from his knitting.

"Haven't seen you in years," his wife Lane said. As dumpy and pale as her husband, her golden hair always looked oily, no matter how often she washed it. She put down her knitting to hug Paix, then pulled back to examine him. "You're looking well."

Lane's parents — cousins on his mother's side — had thrown her belongings into the street when she joined the Bridgers, about the same time Paix had been forced to leave his home too. Paix and Lane had stayed in the room he now shared with Reina for a short time, until he moved into the trainee barracks and she into the home of one of the Bridger widows.

Paix was fond of his cousins, but they were two of the ugliest people he'd ever met. "Are your children well?"

Unfortunately, the children took after them. But the pair beamed. "Very well," Lane said. "We have another grandchild! She's a few months old now!"

"Oh? Congratulations. From whom?"

"Gertie. You know, the one married to the reporter?"

"Gertie ...." Paix vaguely remembered a thin, plain, serious little girl with limp blonde hair. "How old is she now?"

"Twenty," Heap said, not looking up from his knitting.

"It's so lovely to see you married," Lane said, in a tone which said she'd wondered why they hadn't been invited to the wedding. "You two will have adorable children, I'm sure."

A pang of grief: he wanted nothing more than to marry Reina and have children of his own. "Thank you." Paix glanced over at Reina, who smiled at him. "That's very kind."

* * *

At pre-shift briefing, the Commander said, "There's a charity event over at the poorhouse at mid-day. Hanger, Briscola, time your patrol so you're on the east side of your beat then in case there's a call. Pattsz, you'll be in charge of security."

Lead Constable Pattsz got a sour look on his face. He hated anything which made him leave his desk, especially if it meant standing around outside. "Yes, sir."

Paix was glad the poorhouse was on the east side instead of in their beat. Charity events drew Pot rags, beggars, and malcontents for miles around, who often left trash and caused a disturbance. The events were more a nuisance than a help to the folk who actually lived there.

After briefing, Briscola followed him out to the wagons. "So how are we going to do this?"

"You'll see." Paix leaned back as the horses clomped along and thought about it. If they went down 6th Street first then down the row of shops on the Promenade to 1st right away, they should finish the body sweep and the Hedge by mid-day. They'd have to either eat luncheon very early or rather late.

He decided not to mention food. If he did, Briscola would likely want to eat twice.

They signed in at the beat station and went down 6th Street. Most were gone at their day jobs — shop maids or laborers, messenger boys or doing some job for the Family. The smell of bluing wafted along: it was wash day. Several widows along here took in laundry to survive.

Tiny children toddled along tiny porches while their pregnant mothers knitted, or mended, or washed potatoes. The breeze shifted, and the smell of the river blew clean in his face. The day was overcast, foggy, and cold, but Paix felt heartened. He was eight-and-thirty, and still strong, with twenty years on the force. In ten years, he could get a pension.

If Reina's plan succeeded, it might be enough for them to survive. All he had to do was not get killed first.

A pang of grief struck at the thought of leaving the force. Who would care for these people he'd protected all these years, keep them safe, let them live their lives in peace?

Maybe whoever was alive by then would be up to the task.

They turned the corner, strolling along the shops by the boardwalk. Most were still closed, but a few had shopkeepers sweeping the sidewalk or setting out their signs. Across the way, early-riser tourists strolled along, with the inevitable dog or three pulling ahead on their leashes.

At the corner to 1st Boulevard, the six men on Promenade Patrol waved from the wharf across the wide street, where they sat around a white wrought iron table drinking tea. They called themselves Precinct Zero.

Their job was just what it sounded: to patrol the Promenade from 1st Boulevard West to 1st Boulevard East and make sure no one from the Pot intruded upon their betters.

This group patrolled the west side, another patrolled the east. Six men for half of one street.

Paix stood watching carriages go by in either direction. True, it was a long walk to the park holding the immense monument dedicated to Acevedo Spadros I near the quadrant's tip, but police carriages ran along the Promenade every hour — and the chance of violence was a fraction of what he and Briscola faced alone.

Paix pointed down 1st Boulevard. "Which side do you want?"

"I'll take the Hedge," Briscola said.

So after warning Briscola to make sure he searched the bushes clear to the wrought iron, Paix began searching the broken homes for bodies. He found a few families who'd seen better days, but after checking their identification and making sure they were well, he moved on.

Strictly speaking, it was illegal for quadrant-folk to squat here. But if a few days living in these shacks kept a man and his family from having to go to the Pot, it was better to let them stay. The owners of these homes rarely came by to investigate, and if they didn't already have enforcers, they'd call.

He went into a house with a newly downed roof, open to the sky. "Hello," he called. "Is anyone here?"

Paix pulled aside boards to see if anyone lay dead under the fallen roofing. A portion of the home behind this area had its roof intact, so he crunched over pieces of shingle to the door and stepped through.

A hand fell on his shoulder. A familiar voice said, "I thought I'd see you here."

Paix twisted around, heart pounding. Sheinwold stood in front of him.

9

In a flash, Paix dropped into a crouch, his nightstick out. "What do you want?"

Sheinwold held his hands up. He'd been growing a beard. "I didn't do it."

Paix glanced around. A boarded-up window and the door he just came through were the only ways out. Sheinwold stood between him and the door. "And I suppose the bridges are golden and the Pot is too."

Sheinwold seemed crestfallen. And he looked disheveled, which wasn't like him. "For gods' sakes, Hanger. You really think I'd have a gang of kids not old enough to shave ambush you with bricks?" He stared off to the side for a moment, blinking in disbelief. Then he and Paix locked eyes. "That's really what you think of me?"

He did have a point. Sheinwold was a blocked steam pipe, but he wasn't a maniac. "What do you want?"

The man seemed to slump down into himself. "I didn't do this, Hanger. Everyone thinks I did, which is bad enough. Even the lowlifes on Wharf Patrol are giving me the cold shoulder. But now someone's trying to kill me."

Paix felt closed in, trapped. "Let's go outside."

They went back out to the street, Paix keeping Sheinwold in front of him. But Sheinwold wouldn't go past the relative safety of the porch.

"Very well," Paix said. "Who's trying to kill you?"

Sheinwold's face turned evasive.

"I can't help if I don't know what's going on," Paix said. "I'm not entirely convinced I want to help you in the first place."

Sheinwold bristled. "You fucking owe me, Hanger. I got sent

to question Caddy Arrenegada's family the day you were attacked. I didn't tell the Commander about that brick you threw at the kid, even after you pinned this on me. So don't act like you have all the Aces here." After a moment, Sheinwold's shoulders slumped. "You're the only cop in this city I'm fairly sure isn't beholden to a Family."

Paix chuckled. "If you have to ponder that, you're crazier than I thought."

Sheinwold gave Paix a piercing look. "So if I tell you something you're not going straight to Howell?

Paix laughed. "He lived across the street growing up. Doesn't mean he's my friend." They hadn't really been that close even before Paix signed up to the force. Eight Howell's father was an Associate, and all Eighty ever wanted to do with his life was become a Family man. "I don't have a whole lot of time: Briscola will wonder where I am. Maybe you should think about it and get back to me." He walked down the front steps, but didn't put his nightstick away, just in case.

"No," Sheinwold said. "I'll tell you."

Paix turned around to face him, took a couple of steps up, hand on the railing.

Sheinwold said, "I was at this bar ..."

Two and a half years earlier, Sheinwold had been moving stuff for the Spadros Family. Every so often he'd take a bit of Party Time as payment. He stopped at a bar with a truck full of contraband and met a beautiful red-haired girl from Dickens,who brought him to her place upstairs. She was drinking, he was snorting, they were kissing, when all of a sudden she wanted to go out to his truck.

"I was flying high and said, sure, my little chickadee, why not? So we go out to my truck and there's this guy holding the horses' reins." His shoulders slumped. "It was after midnight, and they had me dead to rights with a truck full of high-tech guns." He glanced away, hand on the back of his neck. "They were Feds, Hanger. It was a trap."

Paix blinked. *A woman, with the Feds?* "How high-tech are we talking about?"

"Tommy-guns from Chicago. No ray guns, nothing like that."

So the Spadros Family was stockpiling Tommy-guns. Paix hadn't heard anything about this. "So what happened?"

"They said they could drag me to Hub and charge me with cultural contamination — 10 years minimum — or I could work for them. They wanted to know who in the department worked for which Family. Some investigation or other." He shrugged. "I was reporting in every two weeks."

Albert Sheinwold reports to the Feds? It seemed inconceivable.

"First it was both of them. About a year ago, he disappears, and she won't say where he's gone to. Six months ago, she disappears, and I figure we're done. Three days ago, I get a message that she has to see me right now. When I show up, she tries to kill me."

"What for?"

"I don't know. First I'm set up as dummy for this thing with you and Briscola, then she takes a shot at me." Sheinwold shook his head. "Something's happened. Best I can figure is those two were up to no good."

Paix gaped at him. "What makes you say that?"

"I wasn't the only one working for them. There were others — not cops, guys like janitors, clerks, drivers — from all over the city. A lot of drivers — people forget those speaker horns of theirs go both ways. After they hired me, I followed her until I found as many as I could to figure out what these people were up to. We used to compare notes." He let out a breath. "So after she shot at me I went to warn them. All of them are dead."

Paix thought this sounded fantastical. How could this be happening and he not hear of it? And how did the Feds get into Bridges in the first place? "Was C.K. in on this?"

"No," he said. "Never trusted the guy. I know he's your friend and all —"

Paix wouldn't have trusted C.K. with something like this either. One drunken comment was all it took. "So what do you want me to do?"

"Make sure my wife and kids are okay. First thing I did after she shot at me was to move them to her father's house up on 104th and Bluff." He took out a pad and pencil, wrote an address. "Been scared to go back — I didn't want to lead the crazy bitch to them."

Paix nodded. "Give me the key to your place; I'll go by every so often and make it look like they're at home." From the way he looked, Paix felt sure Sheinwold hadn't been home in a while.

Sheinwold seemed surprised as he handed over the key. "Good thinking."

"Anything else?" Paix wasn't sure why he was helping Sheinwold, but it seemed the right thing to do.

"If you could get some of my clothes and things ...."

Ah. "You're living here."

Sheinwold's cheeks reddened. "It looks bad, but the hot water and stove pipes work. Briscola's too lazy to search all this, and no one else but you would bother. I should be safe enough."

"Never thought I'd be saying this, but I'm glad you're safe."

"Thanks." He turned to go back inside.

"Wait," Paix said. "So what happened to the Tommy-guns?"

"They went missing." Sheinwold shrugged. "I told her where I delivered them. I guess she's got them."

Paix stood for a moment after Sheinwold left. "Strange," he murmured, then continued his search for bodies. He met Briscola three-quarters of the way through.

"What took you so long?" Briscola said.

"More people squatting than usual," Paix said. He didn't think Briscola would be involved in this, but he couldn't be sure. And he didn't want the kid haring off to fight Sheinwold in any case. "Nothing to worry about."

* * *

The crowd around the poorhouse was large enough to see from Snow Street, so Paix and Briscola stood on the corner of 1st and Snow until it began to disperse. Then they returned to the waterfront for luncheon.

"Rough day? It's getting late. Thought I wouldn't see you two," the chili vendor said. He handed them bowls and spoons.

"We got an early start down here," Briscola said. "One of the uppers decided to be charitable."

The vendor snickered, then tipped his hat. "You gents have a good day."

When they sat, Paix said, "It doesn't pay to disparage your betters. You never know who's listening."

"What do you mean?"

"I mean, they're instructed to tell Roy Spadros about comments like the one you just made. We don't know who was over at the poorhouse today."

Briscola stopped chewing. Then he swallowed. "Oh."

"How did you make it to adulthood being so oblivious to your surroundings?"

"Well, I don't know, Constable." Briscola sounded annoyed. "I'll try not to embarrass you further." He began stirring his chili.

Paix let out a breath. "I'd just like you not to find yourself in someone's sights. They might miss."

Briscola grinned at that. "Yeah, they might."

"Would it offend if I asked a personal question?"

Briscola shrugged.

"Why are you here?"

Briscola swallowed a mouthful, wiped his mouth, glanced away. "My Pa died last year —"

Paix felt chagrined. "Forgive me."

Briscola shook his head. "Naw, it's all right. But this pays the best of anything I found so far." He let out a breath. "Pa was never keen on the Families — his grandpa's dad was servant to the Mad King." He glanced away. "Sounded a bit too fond of the old guy for my liking." He took another bite, chewed, swallowed. "Anyway, there's bad blood between him and the Spadros men, and they wouldn't take me, 'cause I'm his son." He shrugged. "Ma hates that I'm a cop. But I got my Ma, two little brothers, and four little sisters to help feed," he gave a wry grin, "so here I sit."

On a Probationary's salary? "An admirable play."

He shrugged. "Made the mistake of telling her how much I made. She won't let me send but half of it, which barely pays what they need. But I give most of the rest to my oldest little sister. She's made a good match; I told her to get whatever she needs for her dower chest and stash it away. My littlest brother's too young to work yet, but the other one stocks shelves for the corner grocery. When he comes up short on hours she slips him a few pennies so we have enough." He grinned. "Ma never knows."

"When's the wedding?"

"End of June, soon as she's of age." He smiled to himself. "Not quite the drunken idiot you imagined, eh?"

Paix chuckled. "I never thought such a thing."

Briscola's cheeks reddened, and he set to finishing his food.

This sounded like a smart play, but Paix considered the mother. "You should tell your mother you're helping your sister with her dowry. What if your mother's lying awake nights worrying about how to pay for it?"

Briscola looked up in alarm. "I never considered it," he said, mouth full. He swallowed. "I'll tell her this weekend."

Paix smiled, clapped him on the shoulder. "Good lad." He checked his pocketwatch. "If you're done here, it's best we were back to work."

* * *

Paix was filling out his reports when Lead Constable Pattsz came by his desk, his jacket already on. "Commander's looking for people to do night duty on Market Center."

Extra night duty was a lot of money. "What, your buddies didn't want to do it?"

"Last time I help you, you ungrateful pin-head." Pattsz glanced away. "Thought you could use the overtime."

Paix grinned."I could." He gathered up his reports and stood. "What day?"

"Saturday, nine to eleven on the Plaza." Pattsz lowered his voice. "We got ten men assigned. There could be trouble."

"What kind of trouble?"

"Fucking Bridgers. One of their gods-damned tent meetings. Commander's angry that the higher-ups approved it, but what can we do?"

"That's fairly remarkable," Paix said. The Commander wasn't known for his temper.

"You could hear him yelling at the poor clerk who brought

the message all the way to my desk." Pattsz paused, hand to his chin. "I don't think he likes the changes around here."

Paix nodded. "Must be hard for these old guys." He patted Pattsz on the shoulder. "You tell the Commander I'll be there."

Pattsz chuckled as he wandered towards the door.

Paix turned in his reports to the front desk. "Any news on the missing boy?"

"Which one? We got six active cases now." The clerk checked his clipboard. "They found Arrenegada, though."

Paix leaned forward. "Caddy? The one who beat me and my partner?"

"Yeah." The clerk peered at the list, flipped to the next page. "Found him dead."

Paix gaped at the man, horrified. "Dead?"

"Yeah. Strangled." He tossed the clipboard aside. "Can't say I'm too surprised. But strangling — what a hell of a way to go."

"Who are the others gone missing?"

The clerk pointed at the missing board. The portraits of Caddy's friends who'd assaulted Paix and Briscola behind the beat station perched along one edge of it beside David Bryce's photo.

Caddy dead. His friends missing. What was going on here?

* * *

Sheinwold's wife was fine, and seemed relieved that her husband was safe. Sheinwold's house had been ransacked. Paix stood in the midst of the mess, puzzled. What could this Fed woman possibly have been looking for?

Paix got some clothes and toiletries together and brought them over. "You got any money? I'll have to get a taxi-carriage back home."

"Sure." Sheinwold handed over a five dollar bill.

"Whoa," Paix said. "This is way too much. You sure?"

Sheinwold got an amused look on his face. "I get tens and twenties from the Family every weekend. But if it makes you feel better, I got this particular fiver from the Wharf Patrol the other day. Besides, you're saving my life. Now here," He pushed the bill forward. "Buy Reina flowers or something."

A five wouldn't get Paix home: a cab driver wouldn't take it. And only the Bank on Market Center would cash such a large bill. But Paix kept a penny in his shoe for just such an occasion. And the five would replace the one he'd given to Howell.

By the time Paix got home, Reina was just starting dinner. Her cheeks were glowing, but she looked tired. Paix put his arms around her. "I see you went to the Plaza. Did it go well?"

She beamed, relaxing into his body. "I never considered how beautiful the place is. And the people! There must have been thousands." She raised her face to his. "It's been a while since I've done so much spinning, though."

No sign of her spinning wheel. She must have left it at the booth: it was heavy and he wasn't there to carry it. "Let me get changed and I'll help."

She kissed him. "I can't tell you how much I love you."

He kissed her forehead. "And I you. But I can't bear to be in this uniform a moment longer."

* * *

The station was in an uproar when Paix walked in the next morning. Groups of men gathered around reading something. Here and there, a group would exclaim, or whistle, or shout.

Paix walked over to Briscola, who sat with his head in his hands. "What's going on?"

"Some pamphlet. I don't know." Another roar of shouts, and pain crossed Briscola's face. "I should not have drunk that much last night."

Paix chuckled, remembering his first months with money and on his own. He clapped Briscola gently on the shoulder. "Pity you're feeling so poorly. And on a work day, too."

Briscola groaned. "You're no help."

They started up on 6th Street this time. The morning was fairly uneventful: rousting a drunken man asleep on the sidewalk (on a Tuesday!); finding a frantic woman's missing toddler (he was asleep under the porch); breaking up a fight between two elderly neighbors who each said the other stole his shovel.

Paix had to whistle for the ambulance on that one, and the

two men were sent to the hospital tied to their cots, still arguing with each other.

When they sat for luncheon, Paix asked, "Whatever happened with your Ma? Did you talk to her?"

Briscola shrugged, not meeting his eye.

A merchant came up to them. "Can you make sure Detective Constable Sheinwold gets it?" He handed Paix a thick money-sized package.

"What the hell is this?" Paix thrust the wad back into the man's hands. "I don't do this kind of work. Besides, who says I know where Sheinwold is?"

The merchant's brown face paled. "Listen, he hasn't come by. I don't want to be late on my fees, you hear?" He glanced around. "I'm not the only one on our block who's worried."

Good gods, Paix thought. "Look. I don't know anything about this. I'm sure the Family'll figure it out for themselves." Paix had no idea Sheinwold was the chip for this area. "You know who's over him? Who he reports to? Send a messenger to fetch the guy, then you can tell him about it."

The man nodded rapidly, eyes darting around. "Yeah. Good idea. Thanks."

"These people are scared as beaten puppies," Briscola said after the man rushed off. "What the hell was Sheinwold doing?"

Paix shrugged. There might be more than one person trying to kill the man. "Let's do the Hedge next."

But when Paix went to where Sheinwold had been staying, the man was gone, along with any trace he'd ever been there.

10

When they turned onto 2nd Street, a figure far down the block was waving wildly at them. Paix and Briscola jogged towards the figure.

"You gotta be careful in situations like this," Paix said, "and don't let your guard down. Stay away from the side alleys. This could be a trap."

Briscola nodded, puffing.

The figure turned out to be a woman: Mrs. Bryce. "You must help me. My boy wasn't here when I woke, and I thought he went looking for work without waking me. But it's almost tea-time! He's never out this late."

Briscola had his back to them, scanning the area.

Paix took a deep breath. *Don't get agitated.* "So your older boy is missing." Paix vaguely remembered the boy: sixteen or so, about as tall as Briscola, with the same pale skin, dark hair, and dark eyes as his mother. "May we come inside?"

Her cheeks flushed, and she glanced away. "Of course."

They stepped into the cold, musty shop. No customers were inside. Paix took out his notebook and pencil. "When did you last see your son?"

"When I went to bed last night."

"When you last saw him, did he say or do anything unusual?"

She peered towards the floor. "He was angry that no one had found David." She raised her head. "No one's even come by!"

C.K. said he would speak with her! He forced his voice to be neutral. "What do you mean?"

"I mean other than you and that wretched detective who tried to bully me, no one's come here. I went to the station, my son went twice. No one will tell us anything!"

Paix shook his head without meaning to. "I'm sorry, mum. You should have been notified of everything." *That was C.K.'s job!*

But that wouldn't help anything. How much should he say? "We've been looking very hard for David, mum. I personally have searched for him past my duty time." It had been three weeks now. Could the boy possibly be alive? "We've not found any —"

Wait, he thought. Might she know something?

Mrs. Bryce leaned forward. "What is it?"

"Do you know a Mr. Kiga?"

A cry burst from her. "Oh, gods. Does he know we're here?"

"He must know you're in the city, mum, but we've not given out any particulars. And the Clubbs refused to send you to him."

She sagged, eyes reddening. "Thank the gods." But then she straightened. "And this inquiry from Mr. Kiga was **after** my son'd been taken?"

Good thinking. "Indeed."

She let out a sigh. "I feel relieved. That man wishes us harm, Constable. But it seems to me if he'd taken David the last thing he'd want is for anyone to connect him to it."

Unfortunately, that was their only real lead.

He got a description of what Herbert might have worn, then said, "I'll speak with Detective Senior Constable Kanhu."

She flinched.

"No, not the one who came before. He's been reassigned. Detective Senior Constable Kanhu is a friend."

This seemed to encourage her. "Thank you, sir. And I'm sorry for the way I behaved the last time you came to call."

Paix gave her a thin smile. "Not at all, mum. Quite understandable." He tipped his hat. "Good day, mum. I'll put in the report about your son — Herbert, is it?"

"Yes, Constable. Thank you."

"Do you have a portrait of him? I'll be sure to return it."

"I do." She ran into the other room, returning with the boy's tintype portrait. "Done the same day as his brother's."

"Thank you, this has been very helpful. If either of them return, please contact us at once." Putting the small portrait in his pocket, Paix and Briscola left, heading for the beat station.

Briscola said, "Why did we not call for a crime scene?"

"He probably got a job," Paix said. "If so, he won't be home until dark. He probably didn't have the money for a messenger. Besides, he's sixteen years old. This is a missing person report, not an abducted child."

They continued along.

"I did talk to my Ma," Briscola said. "She said she was proud of me." The way he said it made Paix think it was the first time she'd said it. And that it meant everything to him. "I understand why we didn't call for a crime scene. But it doesn't seem right. It makes it seem like we don't care about him."

Paix hoped Herbert Bryce really had found a job.

Missing persons were the lowest priority. He'd have the portrait photographed, fill out a report. The report would be filed. If Herbert were very lucky, a KASLOF might be printed, but that would be it. Herbert's photo would go on the Missing Board with everyone else.

If Herbert Bryce hadn't found a job, they might never hear from him again.

* * *

Three women had been found shot in the head, right on the other side of the Pot — to be more specific, placed in plain view of the Rathole, so the east side patrol couldn't miss them.

"Whoever did this was sending a message," Commander Green said.

"Sounds like an execution," Briscola said at the same time.

The Commander said, "You might make detective one day."

The rest of the room laughed.

Briscola turned red.

C.K. belched loudly. "What do we know about them?"

The Commander looked sideways at C.K., then said, "The women haven't been identified. But they dressed too well to be Pot rags."

Paix had heard of the Spadros Family's abuses, but at this, he felt sick. What kind of degenerate would execute women?

Commander Green continued, "My guess is that they were

either maids or molls who upset the Family somehow. Who knows? Maybe they had a three-for-one discount on bullets."

Chuckles ran through the room, but Paix didn't find it funny.

The Commander said, "Kanhu, go check it out."

It was C.K.'s area, but Paix had a pit in his stomach. More distractions for an already overburdened man.

The Commander said, "Hanger, tell us about the missing kid you were called on yesterday. The brother of that first one, right?"

Scattered murmurs.

Paix said, "So he didn't return home."

The Commander reviewed his list. "Not according to night patrol. They went by around midnight; the mother sat outside."

Paix thought about the whole situation. Pursued by a bill collector. Numerous attempts by the family to get answers about the youngest son's disappearance thwarted. The oldest son now gone. "Herbert Bryce went looking for his brother. And whatever happened to David is probably what happened to him."

Commander Green peered at him. "You think they're related."

"I do, Commander."

The Commander sat still for a moment. "See me in my office after briefing. Briscola, take one of those Trainees pretending to file paperwork and start your patrol. Constable Hanger will meet you later."

Paix and Briscola stared at each other, then at the Commander. "Yes, sir," they both said.

After the briefing, Paix followed the Commander to his office. *What kind of trouble am I in now?*

Paix almost felt like laughing at the absurdity of his job. Three women executed rated a detective going to "check it out" as to whether the Family did the deed — in which case it was ignored — but a Constable having an opinion earned a trip to the Office.

They went inside. "Close the door, Hanger."

The Commander sat on the edge of his desk. "I honestly do not know what to do with you."

He paused for so long that Paix thought the man waited for a response. So he said, "Commander?"

This seemed to rouse the Commander from his reverie.

"Would you hazard a guess as to what the east beat detectives learned when they went to notify the Arrenegada family of their son's murder?"

Paix had a guess, but he said, "No, Commander."

"The family told them you threw a brick at their twelve-year-old! And a Spadros Associate's son at that. They want you arrested as a suspect!"

Paix snapped to attention, staring straight ahead. "I did not kill the boy, Commander. I didn't even wish him dead."

"And then you go making some kind of Sherlock Holmes statement in the middle of briefing." The Commander shook his head. "You're a good cop, Hanger. You're clean. And a damn good mind. You should by rights be a Detective."

I was, once — long ago. Refusing to look the other way at a child's murder — a child who'd stolen from the Family — brought that dream to a screeching halt before his career had really begun.

Paix felt surprised the Commander didn't know that. Had they even removed mention of the promotion from his files?

"Half the precinct respects that. The other half thinks you're a danger to the force who's going to bring the whole Family down on us one day. I agree with them both."

The Spadros Family could make life impossible for him personally, but killing a twenty-year veteran would make the rest close ranks. And the Family needed the police to lend legitimacy to their operations. Killing a whole precinct would cause a public outcry — and possibly bring the Feds to the table. "I don't think we need fear that."

Commander Green smiled. "Detective Senior Constable Kanhu needs your help. You need my help. So here's what's going to happen: you help Kanhu with these two cases; I make the brick incident go away."

An astonished glimmer of hope. "Is this a promotion?"

"Hell, no. Are you crazy? You threw a brick at a child! You're not getting more money, Hanger. You're not getting a shield. Be grateful you're not getting fired. You're lucky I don't make you work all day then send you to pull corpses out of the river all night alongside Sheinwold."

Paix peered at the Commander, remembering the merchant's words and the abandoned house. Had someone seen him helping Sheinwold? He had a sudden urge to tell Commander Green that Sheinwold wasn't behind the attack.

But not only did he have no real proof of that, as far as anyone knew Paix had no idea where Sheinwold was. If someone was indeed trying to kill the man, Paix wanted himself, Reina, and his family as far from this as possible.

"Don't look so alarmed, Hanger. You're just out of the hospital and I don't have enough men by half as it is. You're going to help Kanhu on your time, and you'll do your patrol on my time. Keep whatever Trainee Briscola picked to help out."

"Thank you, Commander."

"Have any reporters been asking about these boys?"

"No, Commander."

"Well, if anyone asks, you send them to me. Got it?"

"Yes, Commander."

"Dismissed."

* * *

As Paix suspected, Probationary Constable Briscola and his Trainee were walking 6th Street. Officer Trainee Tanee Lightner was a gangly, dark-skinned young man with big brown eyes and a thick mop of straight black hair.

Briscola relaxed visibly when Paix caught up to them. Lightner seemed nervous — probably his first real patrol — but eager to learn.

As they walked, Paix went over what to look for — things out of place, people acting strangely, unusual smells or noises. "You have brothers and sisters?"

"Yeah," Lightner said. "Four of each."

"Where are you in all that?"

"I'm the oldest."

Paix nodded. And from his accent, Lightner's parents were outsiders. Which made sense. *His parents are probably proud of him,* Paix thought bitterly. "So how do you know if they're doing something they shouldn't?"

Lightner let out a laugh. "They're either making a gods-awful racket or they're too quiet."

Sixth Street was nice to walk early on. The elderly ladies tottering out to say hello, the quiet crisp air. They turned right onto the Promenade, past the shops just starting to open, then right again on 5th Street.

Lightner yawned.

Paix said, "Too early for you?"

"A bit."

Briscola rolled his eyes.

"You'll become accustomed," Paix said. "Or if not, there's always night shift."

Lightner said, "What's night shift like?"

Paix forced himself to walk at the same pace, but his skin crawled at the memories. "Dangerous."

The three walked in silence as the neighborhood stirred around them, the smells of cooking in the air. They turned left on Snow, then left again on 4th.

Footsteps running up behind, several of them.

Paix wheeled around, nightstick out, as four young men wearing black suits and gray tweed caps approached.

"Whoa," one said, drawing back with his hands out as if to push Paix away. "We mean you no harm." The others were bent over, panting.

"Don't run up to police like that," Paix snapped, heart pounding. "What do you want?"

"Mr. Eight Howell invites you to the Backdoor."

They ran five miles to tell him that? Maybe Howell had a lead on the missing boy. "Don't you have bicycles?"

"What do you think we are, messenger boys?" The young man straightened his collar. "We like to keep ourselves fit."

Paix chuckled. "Very well. What time will he be there?"

"Oh, he's always around." They turned and walked off the way they came.

Lightner's eyes were frightened. "You know Eight Howell?"

Paix glanced at Briscola, who was gaping at Lightner. "Sure."

* * *

Paix, Briscola, and Lightner re-canvassed the neighborhood, letting people know about the second missing boy. As usual, no one knew or saw anything. Paix returned Herbert Bryce's portrait to his mother.

After finishing his reports, Paix went by the Backdoor Saloon, which was much busier at six o'clock. The patrons glanced at him as if a policeman strolling in was an everyday occurence.

When Paix said he was here to speak with Eight Howell, the bartender sent a kid of perhaps ten into the back to let him know.

Howell came out scowling at him. "Fucking took you long enough," he said. "We got a problem."

Paix followed Howell into a back office. Dark brown paneling. Portraits of unclad women. Stacks of files and ledgers along the back wall. A big, dark brown desk, with a small electric lamp sitting on it.

Howell shut the door behind them. A black leather chair sat in front of the desk; Howell gestured to it. "Sit," he said; Paix did so. Howell sat in a matching chair behind the desk. "Certain people are very unhappy with you."

"About Caddy Arrenegada."

"Yeah. Now I know you didn't kill the kid, but they want to put you back in the hospital. I would rather they didn't do that."

Paix regarded him. "Why?"

"I don't know. Maybe because you got more courage than any of them. But that's beside the point. Did Sheinwold do it?"

Paix stared at him, startled. "What?"

"Word is the kid framed Sheinwold. Stands to reason he'd want some payback."

"No, I don't think so. Not that I know of." Paix considered this. "I can't see the guy strangling someone." He remembered the Tommy-guns. "Shooting them. Beating them to death, maybe. But strangling a kid?" He shuddered. "I don't think so."

"Yeah," Howell said. "There is that." He sat silent for a moment. "I can protect you —"

Paix waved his hand in front of him, shaking his head. "No. Absolutely not."

"Take it as a favor. I know how much you make — that five

you gave me was much too generous."

"No. No favors." He rose. Favors was the first step on a road which led to working for them. "I'll deal with this on my own."

"See, that's why I respect you." He took out a cigar, lit it. "I tell you what. I'll go to them, tell them we had a little discussion and I don't think you did it."

"Thanks," Paix said.

"It's of no consequence. The kid was a no-good punk, even his dad said so. But he was **their** no-good punk." He puffed at his cigar. "I'll give them your five and tell them you're making amends. They'll settle down." He peered up at Paix. "But if you throw bricks at our kids again, Hanger, there's gonna be trouble."

Remorse flooded through him. I *don't even know why I did it.* "Tell them I'm sorry their boy's dead. I never wanted that."

"Go on," Howell said, but it was kind. "Get out of here."

11

Lightner was on the wagon when Paix rode to the station. Though the other Trainees chattered along, the young man seemed subdued, withdrawn.

Paix yawned, amused. *He must really not like mornings.* This life would cure Lightner of that very quickly.

Where could David and Herbert Bryce have gone? If they were dead, why hadn't anyone found the bodies? If they weren't dead, who was keeping them, and why?

He'd heard nothing from the Cathedral one way or the other. He really didn't want to return there, but it'd been almost a month now with no word.

Sheinwold claimed he went to all the brothels in the Pot, and no one knew anything. Paix wished he would have asked Sheinwold about it when he had the chance.

Where was Sheinwold, anyway? He'd said someone was trying to kill him. Had they succeeded?

Paix doubted the man was dead. There were no signs of a struggle at the ruined house, and Sheinwold was a tough, sneaky survivor.

Anyway, if he were dead, Wharf Patrol would have found his body by now. Criminals tended to be lazy. Why go to the trouble of digging a grave when you could tie a chunk of rubble to someone's ankle and dump them off a pier?

If Sheinwold were still a regular cop, Paix could see someone taking the trouble to bury him. Cop-killing was unforgiveable to other cops, even if done by the Family. Now that he'd been kicked down to Wharf Patrol, though, he was fair game.

Paix hoped Sheinwold was alive.

The morning was quiet. A woman who didn't know where to

buy a new bed was directed to the shop on 10th Street. A three-year-old wandering in the middle of 6th Street was escorted home. Her mother was drunk, sleeping on the floor beside their battered sofa.

Paix fixed the girl porridge while the other two patrolmen chatted with her, warning the child to stay inside until her mother woke up. Then they placed the woman on her sofa. Paix left a citation on the table: her third that he knew of. The carbon copy would be put into her file.

"This seems pretty easy," Lightner said as they walked down the front steps. "But I never knew you had to feed children before." He said it as if this changed the way he thought about his whole situation.

Briscola grunted.

"Walk up ahead for a bit, tell me what you see," Paix said to Lightner. When he did, Paix stopped, turning to Briscola. "Are you well? You've hardly said a word since shift started."

"I don't like this guy being here," Briscola said.

Paix let out a surprised laugh. "You picked him."

"I know, but — oh, I don't know. I liked it better when it was just us two."

Paix grinned, patting Briscola on his shoulder. "He's only here a few weeks. Then you'll have me all to yourself."

Briscola shied away, face red. "Hell, it's not like I'm sweet on you or nothing."

"It's perfectly normal to react when things change. Just don't let it interfere with your work." Paix glanced around. "Don't forget where you are."

They walked up to Lightner, who'd been studying the area. "I don't see anything."

"Really," Paix said. "Nothing?"

"Old houses, bushes." He paused, scuffing the ground with a shoe. Then he pointed. "That one's missing shingles."

"That's good," Paix said, and they continued walking. "You need to know what the usual is before you know if something's out of place. That house with the missing shingles is empty; Party Timers like to light up there nights. Once in a while we'll get called during the day because one of them broke into another house and stole something. Or they'll run out when we walk by saying one of them's dead. If there's enough complaints, the Commander will tell us to arrest the ones with identification papers and toss the rest into the Pot. But that roof's been missing those shingles for a while now."

Lightner said, "So if you know they've got Party Time on them, why don't you go in there and arrest them now?"

Briscola snapped, "How long you been in this city, outsider?"

Lightner bristled. "All my life. We live on Market Center."

Paix raised a hand. "Settle down, Briscola." He said to Lightner, "What do your parents do?"

Lightner scowled. "My mother has a booth on the Plaza, next to your wife," he said to Paix. "I saw you there with them the other day. Is that why you're stuck in Precinct 1? Because you're a fucking Bridger?"

Paix laughed at the notion. "We aren't Bridgers. The people who own that shop are my first cousins once removed on my mother's side. They're letting her spin for them."

So that's why this guy's been brooding. "The answer to your other question is just as simple. We don't arrest them now because they're Spadros men. Wastrels, most of them, but still Family men. The Family pays them in Party Time and saves their cash to build useless mansions." He kicked a small rock, which went skittering down the cracked sidewalk. "The Spadros Family doesn't take kindly to us arresting their men every day."

I wish we could, though. Get them off the streets and out of our city. "Anything else you'd like to know?"

Lightner hesitated, then glanced away. "No," he said angrily.

Paix considered the time the Trainee had been with them, and his reactions. "You've had trouble with Eight Howell."

Lightner wheeled, lunging towards him. "You're damn right I have. The bastard killed my father, right in front of me. And now I learn you work for him."

Paix put his hand on Lightner's chest. "Whoa," Paix said. "I don't work for Howell. We grew up together." He dropped his hand to his side. "I'm sorry about your father."

"Yeah," Lightner said bitterly, turning away. Then the tension seemed to drain from him. "We should never have come here."

They kept walking. Paix felt glad the cards were all out on the table. Maybe now the kid could learn something.

A woman's scream from the other side of the block. "Help! Help me!"

Paix drew his nightstick, leading the men through the narrow space between two houses and past a fetid back alley.

When they emerged upon 3rd Street, an older olive-skinned woman stood on the front porch in her house dress, her face streaked with tears. "My husband's fallen!"

They rushed inside: a dark-skinned old man lay on the floor clutching his chest, his face sweaty and ashen, twisted in pain. "Call the ambulance," Paix told Briscola, who ran outside, Lightner running after him. The series of whistles rang loud and shrill above the woman's sobbing.

"I can't breathe," the man said. "Oh, gods, it hurts."

Paix knelt at the man's head and supported his head and upper shoulders with his knees. "Take off his shoes, put his feet up," he told the woman, who rushed to help. "Does he have medicine for this?"

The woman shook her head.

"Be at peace," he said to the man. "The hospital-men are on their way."

"It's so hard to breathe." The man gave Paix a pleading look. "Am I dying?"

"I'm not a doctor. But I've seen men survive this."

Lightner ran back inside, frantic. "What shall I do?"

"Calm yourself," Paix said, "so as not to agitate matters. Ask Probationary Constable Briscola to whistle once more. Be ready to direct the ambulance-men here."

Lightner took a deep breath, and his eyes lost some of their wildness. "Yes, sir. Constable." He ran back outside.

The wife clutched her husband's hand. "Oh, Harold," she sobbed. "I'm so sorry we argued."

Harold smiled over at her with bluish lips, his eyes showing the pain he faced. "Don't berate yourself." He clutched his chest again with a moan as he looked up at Paix. "How much longer will it last?"

Paix brushed gray curls off Harold's forehead. "It won't be long now, sir."

"You've done well, Constable," Harold whispered. His eyes went to his wife. "I love you so much." A few moments later, he began gasping.

Paix sat with Harold and his weeping wife as the gasps moved further apart, then stopped. Lightner stared at them, arms crossed, until the ambulance-men galloped up.

Then Paix closed Harold's eyes. "May he be dealt better cards next time."

The ambulance-men brought Harold out wrapped in a sheet. His wife followed behind, a shawl around her bent shoulders. "Thank you," she said, then climbed up to sit with him.

As the ambulance drove off, Lightner began sobbing, face in his hands.

Paix glanced at Briscola, who looked away, then put his arm around Lightner's thin shoulders. "This is part of the job as well."

Lightner nodded. "Yes, Constable." He calmed himself, wiped his eyes on his sleeve. "Was there nothing we could do?"

"If he had medicine for his heart, perhaps. They say we used to be able to treat such things better."

Briscola said bitterly, "I heard they have better doctors in Azimoff. More ambulances. Better medicine. Why do **we** have to watch men die?"

Paix shrugged. The Cultural Correctness Committee — which forbade every technological advance — had much to answer for. And Bridges, which put such low value on these people's lives. And the Spadros Family itself, which interfered with the police in their quadrant at every turn.

If we had even our own wagons, we could carry medicine for these men. But they always claim there's no money.

* * *

As Paix sat typing his reports that evening, his mind drifted back to Herbert and David Bryce. He went to the front desk:

neither boy had been found. Nor had any of Caddy's friends.

Something about this didn't feel right.

After Paix turned in the reports, he went to C.K.'s desk. Stacks of files were piled on the floor on either side. It took a while, but Paix found the files for Herbert and David Bryce then returned to his desk with a cup of tea.

Paix felt sure Herbert Bryce had gone looking for his brother. Which implied Herbert thought he knew where David might be.

But where would Herbert go?

There were even fewer clues to Herbert's case than his brother's. The night shift's second canvass the night earlier had found a neighbor who said the boy came asking for money to help find his brother. That sounded like Sheinwold's doing.

Why didn't the night shift put that in this morning's briefing?

They might not have finished their reports in time for the information to have made it to the Commander, Paix decided. He noted the neighbor's name, the address, and the file number, then put the note in his desk. He wouldn't be able to talk to the man until Monday, but maybe Herbert said something else to him which might be helpful.

"Hey, Constable," Briscola said. "We're going out for drinks. Want to come along?"

"No," Paix said. "But thanks for asking."

Another Probationary walked past, giving Paix a leering grin. "He's got sweet little side bet, I hear."

At the man's tone, Paix stood. "Probationary Constable, over here now."

The man came over. "Yeah?"

Paix felt annoyed. "Yes, Constable."

"Yes, Constable."

"You speak of a respectable woman, Probationary Constable, and you will refer to her as such."

From his breath, the man had begun drinking hours ago. "Can't be too respectable, now, Constable. From what I hear, she was your partner's wife, now she's with you."

"The private business of Constables is none of your concern."

The man rolled his eyes. "If you say so. Constable."

Paix could put the man on report. But he didn't know what his connections were. "Dismissed."

The man threw a scrap of paper on Briscola's desk. "We'll be there tonight."

"Sorry about that, sir," Briscola said once the man left. "That one's a right bastard."

"Family man?"

Briscola gave Paix a sharp, surprised glance. "His brother just made Associate. How'd you know?"

Paix shrugged. It seemed obvious from the man's behavior, from his sauntering through the precinct drunk to his manner with a superior. The Probationary felt himself untouchable.

12

On the way home, Paix came to a decision: he wasn't giving the Family a five dollar bill ever again. He stopped by the bank just before it closed and broke the fiver in his secret pocket.

Paix and Reina had a leisurely dinner, then he handed her one of the dollars. "I want you to go to that apothecary and set up an account to get the blood tea. I don't want you to ever go through this again."

She smiled, blushing. "I will."

"Are you fit for the tub?" Reina had said the apothecary forbade her to sit in water until her bleeding had stopped.

Reina considered this. "I am."

"I feel relieved," Paix said. "Tonight, I shall draw us a bath. Then I shall brush your hair and love you as you deserve."

Paix woke curled on his side to the warm sound of dripping. Reina hummed a quiet tune from behind. The midday light streamed in the open window; the air felt humid and smelled of soap. He smiled to himself. "Thanks for washing my uniform."

He rolled over. His uniform hung on the far end of the clothes rack, where it dripped into a metal pan.

Reina stood in the kitchen pressing the pants of his second uniform. She returned the iron to the stove, put down her hot pad, and came over to sit beside him. "Sleep well?"

He stretched, savoring how rested he felt. "I did." He yawned, rubbed his eyes. "I thought you'd be at the Plaza."

"Since you have duty tonight, I told Lane I'd help her at the booth while you're at work. We can go home together."

It sounded like a good idea, but — "Only if you promise not to visit. There's been word this meeting could turn ugly, and I don't want you anywhere nearby."

"Heap said the same thing. Lane wanted to close the booth. Yesterday, they argued over it."

Paix had forgotten this was a Bridger meeting. But why close their booth on the best sales night of the week? It made no sense. "Do they have to go to every meeting?"

Reina smiled at him. "Gertie's husband is speaking."

"Oh!" Paix said. Of course Lane would want to see her son-in-law speak. "I should be pleased to meet him." He considered the night to come. "If there's trouble, I might not be done until late."

"I can go home with Heap and Lane; I'll leave a note at the booth if we do."

She'll be safe with them, he thought.

"Hungry? One of the butchers at the Plaza had some smoked bacon that didn't sell, and he gave me a good price."

Paix dressed in comfortable house clothes and made the bed while Reina finished pressing his pants. She hung the pants up next to his second jacket and his uniform shirts, then put the leftovers from dinner into the oven. He began slicing the lump of smoked bacon into strips. "Sounds as if you're selling well."

"I've never seen two people so in love with knitting," Reina said. She set the iron aside to cool. "They're buying yarn from a dozen spinners, and if they didn't have to take money, eat, and sleep, I don't think they'd do much else."

That made Paix chuckle. Heap and Lane were perfect for each other. "She made that coverlet during the six weeks she stayed here." He put his knife down and pointed to their knitted bedspread. "And that was twenty years ago. I'm sure she's much faster at it now."

"She is," Reina said. "It's amazing."

Paix lay the sliced bacon in the skillet, where it began to sizzle. With their leftovers from dinner, it made a fine meal.

How fortunate I am to be here, away from the Families, with a woman who loves me.

After eating, Paix lay on the bed as Reina washed the skeins of yarn she'd made that week and hung them to dry.

Monday, he'd speak with that neighbor about Herbert Bryce.

Hopefully C.K. would be around and they could discuss Herbert and David's cases for a few minutes. Even though he'd been in the force less time than Paix, C.K. had been a detective for over fifteen years. He was bound to have some notion of where to look next.

The afternoon sun streamed in the window warm upon his legs, and a cool dry breeze entered which felt refreshing. It wasn't often he had time to relax, and Paix savored it.

Reina turned from where she'd hung the last of this week's skeins. "Ten. That's the most I've ever done in a week."

"Congratulations."

She came over and sat beside him. "I'll probably spend much of my time tonight carding. The wool Heap got for me to spin is dirty and matted, a huge bag of it."

Paix glanced over at the wash water, which was a dark brown. "How much are they paying you per skein?"

"Five cents, but —"

"Only five?" Paix didn't know how much yarn went for, but it seemed too much work for fifty cents a week.

"Yes." She put her hand on his arm. "But it's fifty cents more than we had." She took his hand and kissed it. "And it's a step in the door." She lay down beside him. "I think they're trying to help us. Their hats and scarves don't sell for much more than that. I think if they dyed the yarn different colors it might help. But Heap says that's unnatural." She fell silent.

"My cousins are certainly strange," Paix said. "I don't know to this day what possessed Lane to join up with the Bridgers. Wasn't for lack of asking." He turned to face her, sliding his arm under her neck. "Or marry that man Heap. His face would stop a clock!"

Reina chuckled. "She's married someone who's shared her life. Who loves the same thing she does. It's rare." She fell silent for several moments. "I think she's done very well, under the circumstances."

Paix considered the matter. "I don't understand."

Reina propped her head up on an elbow to face him, moving his arm away. "Have you ever seen a less attractive woman? She'd never get a husband unless she joined the Bridgers. But she took heed of the cards she'd been given and made a smart play. Now she's a booth owner with children and grandchildren, while other more beautiful women die lonely spinsters." She paused for a moment. "I admire her courage."

Paix rolled on his back. "I never considered this before." It made him rethink many things. Could it be his cousin never truly believed in the Bridger way? "It seems so," he hesitated, searching for the right word, "calculated."

Reina smiled, brushing a lock of hair from his forehead. "Women have fewer choices, my love, and those choices are often a matter of life and death."

For tea-time, they decided to bake biscuits with chopped bits of the last of their dried fruit mixed in. As they sat drinking tea, Paix examined one. "They turned out well. We should make these again."

A knock at the door.

Alarmed, Paix went for his nightstick. "Who is it?"

"It's Cartas Kanhu, you nit."

Paix laughed, putting aside the nightstick. He opened the door. "You gave me a fright. No one ever comes here."

C.K. looked dressed for work, down to dress shoes and pocketwatch, but he was sweating. "I can see why. Devilishly long climb." He paused, glancing between Paix and Reina. "Hello, Mrs. Bower. May I enter?"

Paix moved aside, suddenly glad he'd made the bed. "We're having tea. Please join us." He gave C.K. the chair, sitting on the corner of the bed with his cup. "What brings you here?"

C.K. chuckled. "Can't let a man drink his tea in peace, eh? We'll have plenty of time to discuss that later."

"If you wish," Paix said, mystified. C.K. had never come here in the entire time they'd known each other. And for the first time in a while, C.K. seemed sober. "I hope your family's well?"

"As well as ever," C.K. said, then took a bite of biscuit. "This is quite good," he said to Reina.

Paix and Reina chuckled, giving each other a glance. Why did the man not come to the point?

"Thank you," said Reina. "We made them together. The fruit

was his idea."

"Doesn't surprise me," C.K. said, his mouth full. Then he swallowed. "Never quite met someone like your fellow here, before or since."

"Well, I hope that's a good thing," Paix said. The sun dipped low, and he had to sit a bit to his right to keep its glare from blinding him.

C.K. snorted. "Likewise." He drained his cup, poured part of another, then stared into the teapot. "Lemme fill this up for you."

Paix watched C.K. fill the teapot from the larger kettle on the stove with amusement. "You look as if you've caught some work."

Then a horrible thought appeared as C.K. turned towards him. The two men's eyes locked, and Paix knew the truth. "You found the boy dead."

C.K. came over, set the teapot down, sat, finished filling his cup, then said, "Yes, we did."

Reina gasped, hands to her mouth. "Oh, Paix, I'm so sorry."

Paix had a terrible vision of little David Bryce lying dead. "The poor child. I should have guessed it, him being gone so very long. Any idea when it happened?"

C.K. peered at him. "Oh. No, not the little one. The oldest boy." He glanced at Reina. "We should discuss the particulars on the way."

Paix blinked. "You want me to inform the mother." He rose. "I'll get dressed right away."

"Sit down, Hanger," C.K. said. "You're on night duty. We'll finish tea like civilized folk and let the poor woman have another hour to hope her son still lives. It's the least we can do for her."

Paix and Reina clasped hands tightly for a full minute as C.K. drank his tea. Paix wanted nothing more than to leap up and force him to reveal every detail. He wanted to rush to the woman's home. But as time passed, he realized that C.K. had the right of it. Nothing they did would bring Herbert Bryce back to his mother, and she deserved to have her tea in peace.

"I suppose I should have waited to come here until after tea-time," C.K. finally said. "I've spoilt your afternoon."

13

C.K. told Paix all about Herbert Bryce's death as they walked down the stair. "Strangled, with one of those Red Dog cards in his breast pocket."

"Why — how would children do such a thing?"

C.K. stopped on the stair, looking up back over his shoulder, his round face lit by the lamp at the top of the stair behind them. "Wasn't children, at least not if the message I got was true. " He continued on down the stairs. "We should examine the body before going to the mother."

Paix followed him. "So Wharf Patrol found him last night?"

"No, it was a Constable walking his beat." C.K. looked back at Paix, this time silhouetted by the lamp at the bottom of the stair. "East beat, east side, 1st Boulevard, Diamond quadrant. Across from the Hedge, but on the sidewalk. Like whoever did this brought his body in a carriage and dumped him there."

Diamond quadrant? What was Herbert Bryce doing there?

"Yeah. Right across the river." C.K. kept going down the stair. "They found him first thing this morning; when the coroner's men got to the morgue, the attendant remembered seeing him on the KASLOF flyer. Took them a while to move the body to Spadros."

They came out into the street in early twilight; the lamps were just being lit. "This is incredible," Paix said.

"Indeed." C.K. flagged down a police wagon. "Spadros morgue," he told the driver. C.K. and Paix got inside and shut the door. C.K. said, "You want to know what else is odd? The boy isn't wearing the clothes in the description."

Gone three days, or perhaps two. "Could he have planned to leave, brought clothes with him? No, the mother said nothing was missing." He peered at C.K. "What does it mean?"

"It means someone was with Herbert Bryce, someone who fed him, gave him clothes. We find that person, we find the man who killed him."

* * *

Paix was all too familiar with the Spadros morgue, but hadn't been there since he was a Detective Constable. The place had changed little. Dreary, cold, the smell of death in the air.

"The clothes are too good to be his," Paix said upon uncovering Herbert's body. "He wore mourning, but that of a mid-quadrant merchant's son. This is fine work."

"See how loosely these hang on him?" C.K. fingered the boy's lapel. "This was made for someone of a similar height but bigger in body. More muscular, I'd wager." He tugged at the boy's belt, but gently. "See how slender the waist? No fat man could wear this." The jacket, a rich brown, was top-stitched in brass thread. "A bit of a dandy, I'd say, and a well-to-do one at that."

Paix loosened the boy's collar. Bluish finger-marks stood plainly on Herbert's pale skin. "A man did this, not a boy."

"So we have the height and build of this man," C.K. mused. "And the size of his hands. Now to find his face."

Paix looked at Herbert's hands, his feet, his face. The arms of his jacket. Nothing. He went to the boy's shoes, which sat on the counter: scuff marks on the back of the heels. He showed them to C.K.. "Looks like he was dragged a bit, but didn't fight much."

"I'd expect it," C.K. said. "This all points to someone luring this boy, probably with the hope of finding his brother. Herbert Bryce was taken in somewhere, given fine clothes, and when the scoundrel finished his sport, he surprised the boy with a strangle." C.K. shook his head. "This is a bad one, Hanger."

The way C.K. said it seemed to imply more than just the horror of a young man being strangled to death. "How so?"

"Caddy Arrenegada's body looked almost identical. I'll have to measure the marks to be sure, but I think this is the same man." C.K. leaned his hands on the edge of Herbert's slab. "And if he likes strangling, he's not going to stop until we stop him."

14

It was after seven before they got to Mrs. Bryce's shop, and it took a few knocks to get her to answer the door. Even so, she peered out as if frightened. "Who is it? What do you want?"

"It's Constable Hanger. I'm sorry to bother you so late, mum. I have news about your son Herbert."

She didn't move, her eyes huge in the darkness. "What news?"

C.K. said, "May we come in?"

Her eyes darted to C.K., and Paix said, "This is Detective Senior Constable Kanhu. The one I told you about. We've been investigating David and Herbert's disappearances."

This seemed to shake her, and she opened the door, moving aside. "Of course. Come in."

The fabric store was dark, but a lone oil lamp burned in the back room, and the men followed Mrs. Bryce to it.

She faced them, wringing her hands. "What's happened?"

Paix moved closer, so as to be able to catch her should she faint. "We've found Herbert, mum. Dead."

She didn't faint, or even cry, just stared at him.

He held out a card. "The address and viewing hours for the morgue. They can help with the arrangements as well."

Her eyes dropped to the card for several seconds, then she took it, putting it in a pocket.

C.K. said, "Is there someone you can call? To be with you."

She stared at him a long moment, then nodded.

C.K. handed her a penny. "For the messenger."

Her mouth dropped open, then she took it. "Thank you."

"Did you have any questions for us? Before we go."

Mrs. Bryce cleared her throat. "How did he die?"

Paix said, "He was strangled. We're on the hunt for his killer."

She stared at him. "Who would want to murder my son?"

Paix shook his head. "We don't know, mum. But we're searching for the scoundrel."

She nodded slowly, not looking at them, then turned away. "Thank you for finding my boy."

Paix and C.K. shared a glance. Paix said, "Would you like us to wait until your friend arrives?"

"No," Mrs. Bryce said. "That won't be necessary." She simply stood there, facing away, without a sound.

After a few moments, Paix said, "Good night then."

She didn't answer, and after a few moments, they let themselves out.

* * *

When they got back to the station, Paix and C.K. split ways. C.K. had reports to add to Herbert's file — which was now a Homicide rather than a Missing Person. Paix took the police wagon to the Plaza. He still had his night duty to do.

The Plaza was a truly immense field covering much of the south end of the island. On the Plaza's north, south, and west sides, six rows of open-air booths constructed of oak beams and roofed well were set upon bases of red brick twenty feet long and wide, with ten feet between each booth on all sides.

Within this array lay a variety which stupefied the mind. Every sort of food or drink, items for homes, gardens, bodies. Carnival games, strolling minstrels, and raised stages featuring various events throughout the day gave the scene a festive air.

Most booths were curtained in thick gray wool felt pulled tight on one or more sides, to keep out the weather, to offer privacy, or to improve the appearance. It wasn't unheard of for men running their booths alone to live in them. Some curtains were embroidered with the sign or slogan of the company within.

People teemed at this hour on a Saturday: children rode their fathers' shoulders, lovers strolled arm in arm, women picked over produce or bargained with sellers. A lamp perched on the outside corner of each booth, and a lamp was embedded in the inside peak of each roof.

Heap and Lane's booth was in the north-west section of the Plaza, on the outer row, across from the Market Center police station. Several people examined the knitted items: baby sweaters, socks, gloves. Lane spoke with a customer while Heap knitted. Reina sat with a huge bag of what looked like old matted hair, using what looked like two rectangular paddles with fine teeth on them to comb through clumps of it. Paix had no idea why they called the things cards, although they were the right shape for it.

Reina put them down when she saw him, dusted herself off, and came over to him with a smile. "You're here! I was wondering if you'd end up having to go straight over."

Paix checked his pocket-watch. "I can't stay long; I have to report in at nine." He surveyed the booth. Reina's spinning wheel stood in a corner behind the tables, a curtain pulled tight behind that keeping anyone from taking it. "Are you selling well?"

Lane glanced over at them. "Well enough," Reina said. "A lot of people like to look first."

Heap put his knitting into a woven bag and stood. "Shall we walk over together?"

Paix felt surprised. "Certainly, sir." He squeezed Reina's hand. "I'll return as soon as I can."

The two men made the long journey towards the Field through the crowds, past booths, then onto the Field itself. Neither spoke as they walked through the clear chill darkness.

After close to an hour's silence, Heap said, "I wish to speak to you on a matter."

Paix figured as much. "By all means."

"This — liaison — you have with Mrs. Bower is not only illegal but immoral," Heap said. "While I'm not inclined to deny her employment, I feel concern for her welfare." He turned, grabbed Paix by the arm. "You risk not only your cards by this reckless play but hers, and the fate of all who receive them in the future. I beg you to reconsider."

Paix let out a breath. How did Heap learn the truth? "Sir, I know your words come only from the best of intention, and I love you for it. But our liaison, as you call it, is voluntary, and welcome to us both."

"But what damage is done?" He turned away for a moment, then shook his head. "I have said my piece. Let us be off."

A large tent approached in the distance, close to the river across the darkened field to the east, its lamplit canvas glowing brightly from inside. Past the tent and across the river, the lights of the Clubb Promenade glowed in the far distance. The canvas stopped at perhaps mid-thigh, and men moved around in and out.

As the lit tent grew larger, Paix thought of Jake: his grief, which turned to obsession and the destruction of his marriage.

Jake and Paix been friends from the day they met. They felt the same way about the Families. They'd been assigned as partners, made Detective together. They'd saved each others' lives so many times. Yet in a moment, it was as if none of it happened.

Why did Jake blame **him** for Reina walking away?

I'm not responsible for their relationship. She came to me.

But then he thought of Lane, and of Reina's words earlier: *Women have fewer choices, my love, and those choices are often a matter of life and death.*

Jake Bower seemed a good man: a hard-working provider, patient, most always cheerful. And a quick mind. He claimed he never raised a hand to her. And it seemed inconceivable that he'd dally with other women. What really happened between Jake and Reina Bower to make her leave him?

* * *

On arriving at the tent, Paix went to the Sergeant Constable assigned to cover security and was ordered to cover the perimeter.

"The speaker is my cousin's husband," Paix said. "Might I greet him?"

The Sergeant Constable, a squat, olive-skinned man, glared at him. "If you're quick about it."

So Paix strode down the center aisle past the many rows of dark wooden folding chairs to the front, where men hammered together a raised stage. Heap stood in front of it, talking with a young man and woman of about twenty.

The young woman had to be Gertie: Paix recognized her by her eyes. The thin, plain girl was now a stout woman whose thin face seemed to have grown wrong: eyes too close together for beauty, teeth protruding and uneven, and she'd inherited Lane's lank, oily-looking hair. But the pride in her eyes for the young man beside her made Paix stop in his tracks.

Reina never looked at him that way.

The man seemed quite ordinary: thin, a shock of straight straw-colored hair, very dark eyes. Their eyes met, and Heap turned to follow. "Oh, here," Heap said, "come over. Mr and Mrs. Thrace Pike, meet your cousin, Master Constable Paix Hanger."

While technically correct, Paix ceased to be called "Master" Hanger when he joined the force at eighteen. He suspected Heap used the word to signal that Paix had never married, should the couple see Paix and Reina together in the future. A sly trick, but one Paix couldn't challenge the man on: he'd claim he was only being polite.

Paix shook Thrace Pike's hand, and Gertie curtsied as he kissed hers. "A pleasure to meet you both," Paix said. "I'm stationed outside should you need assistance."

"We're most grateful, Constable," Thrace said.

"Until we meet again, sir, madam," Paix said, and left the way he came.

The clock tower struck nine. The ten policemen — most of them fat Lead Constables — met together to one side in front of the tent as the first people began arriving, some carrying large boxes of what appeared to be pamphlets.

"All right, men," the sergeant said. "Those I've assigned to perimeter, stay there unless you hear the whistle. Now these are Bridgers," he gave Paix a sharp glance, "so be ready for anything. We don't want no trouble here, so no beating without provocation. But if there is trouble, you get on top of it. We got a chain wagon on standby, along with extra handcuffs." As if on cue, the jingle of the horses' warning bells came from far behind the tent as the wagon approached. "Bring everyone involved into the station, and let the gods-damned Families sort it out."

Paix snorted quietly. He was beginning to like this sergeant.

The sergeant let the perimeter men choose their positions. Paix chose an area to the right of the tent opening, where he could see the river. Several light posts stood there unlit, and he lingered by one. From here, Paix could see the Promenade if he turned one way, and if he turned the other way, the people straggling across the Field to the tent.

The ones going to the tent seemed to be lowers: factory-men, widows, laborers. The Bridgers always drew this sort: discontented because they weren't benefiting from the way things were. Which made the Bridgers' strict ways likely seem a rock they could cling to.

A few of the men he'd seen in the Backdoor Saloon went past. What were they doing here? Paix wondered if these men were the "trouble" they'd been warned to expect. They didn't notice him, and he didn't move towards them.

Soon enough, the tent filled and the stragglers stopped coming. The night was quiet and clear, the noise and lights of the Market far in the distance. On nice nights like this, the tour companies ran their zeppelins for the outsiders; several floated in the distance under the faint shimmer of the dome.

Paix was too far away to hear what Thrace Pike was saying, but after a while, it seemed people weren't too happy with it. A man shouted above the din, then an angry crowd began leaving.

He didn't agree with most of the things the Bridgers believed, but for an instant, Paix felt sorry for the thin young man Lane's daughter had married. He knew what it was like to be scorned for what you believed to be right.

A whistle split the air, and Paix hurried over, scanning for danger as he went. He strode in, and his eye immediately went to a young widow woman who acted furtive. She ducked under the canvas and was gone.

But Paix wasn't there to apprehend odd young widows: a full-out brawl went on in front of the stage. He grabbed a man pummeling a younger one by the back of his jacket, pulling him aside. "Stop this."

The younger fellow lunged forward. Paix stopped him with one hand on his chest, pulling out his nightstick with the other. "You want a beating? Because I can oblige."

All around them, officers were pulling men from the melee.

The man in front of him — perhaps nineteen years of age with blood on his face and a black eye — backed off, hands up. The other had vanished.

Paix said, "Go on, get out of here, before I arrest you."

There were still ten men fighting, but after the police started applying their nightsticks, the men surrendered. Soon a line of policemen with handcuffed men headed around the tent towards the chain wagon.

Paix liked chain wagons, because you got your handcuffs back as soon as you'd chained the man to the handcuffs attached to the wagon's wall. He still had to go to the station to file a report, but he'd get done and home quicker this way.

The wagon-driver whistled: they were boarded up and ready to go.

Paix hoped Thrace, Gertie, and Heap hadn't been hurt, but he didn't want to miss the wagon. So he climbed on the sideboard and grabbed the railing at the top along with the rest, perched around the outside of the wagon as they rode back to the station.

While Paix typed his report on the night's activities — sitting at someone else's desk in the Market Center station — a large man walked past, carrying a thick envelope. Something about him looked familiar.

The man went to the front desk, then after a bit of flurry, he was escorted upstairs.

Paix kept typing. Where did he know the man from?

After a few minutes, the man returned, standing by the front desk as if waiting. Tall and muscular, wearing a topper and fine suit, he was perhaps eight and twenty, but held himself with an air of dignity and power. The rooms where the men were held began opening, the men pouring out.

Those were the men they'd just arrested!

Paix gestured to a Constable passing by. "Who is that man? The big one."

"They call him Sawbuck," the Constable said. "Right hand to the Spadros Heir. Sent to fetch the Family's dogs, I gather."

The man seemed young for such a position. "Figures. I haven't yet finished my reports." Paix glanced around the room;

the other men typing away glanced back. The looks on their faces said they were thinking the same thing.

By the time Paix had finished his reports, it was close to midnight. Since the Plaza closed at eleven, Paix headed to Heap and Lane's home, on the north end of the island. Fortunately, one of the police wagon's drivers agreed to take him there.

Heap answered the door. "Come in," he said.

Lane's home had a few more rooms than his did, but they were small, full of clutter, and untidy. Paix wondered at having six children in a place like this. Reina sat in an overstuffed chair, and lifted her head sleepily when he arrived. "Oh, good, you're not harmed."

Lane peered at her. "Are you sure you won't stay here?"

Reina smiled, but it was forced. "I'm sure." She rose. "Come on, Paix, let's go home."

It was a half mile home, but they walked the empty streets rather than spend the penny on a taxi. Paix asked, "Did they bother you?"

Reina sighed. "I should never have expected this to go well. As soon as I arrived today, a friend came by the booth, calling me Mrs. Bower. It went poorly thereafter."

Paix patted her hand. "I'm sorry. Heap lectured me as we walked. But he said he didn't want to sack you."

"I suppose that's something," Reina said. "Perhaps they'll forget the whole thing."

Somehow, Paix doubted it.

* * *

On Monday, Paix, Briscola, and Lightner had just begun their patrol when a messenger boy rode up, pointing at Paix. "You're wanted at the beat station," the boy said, then rode off.

Paix said, "You two carry on, I'll see what this is about and meet you later."

At the beat station, the sergeant and a wagon stood outside. "Detective Senior Constable Kanhu would like a word with you at the precinct."

"What about?"

"Not my business. Best you be off."

So Paix got into the wagon, which started away.

He found C.K. in one of the interrogation rooms with a blond young man, fourteen or so. "Hello," Paix said to the boy, then turned to C.K.. "You wanted to see me?"

"Sit down." C.K. smelled of alcohol already. "I've got someone here you'll want to meet."

The young man's name was Stephen Rivers. He'd come in because of a man following him. "Tall he was, and dressed a gentleman, all in brown." Stephen's eyes darted to the door, and his hands shook. The boy was missing a small finger.

Paix leaned forward. "What did he look like?"

"Big. He scared me, he did."

"What color hair?"

"I don't know. Brown?"

"What were his eyes like?"

The boy's hands shook more. "They frightened me, sir. He's followed me all over. I've got to go out. I run papers to the doors for the afternoon edition, tuppence a day up front. I can't stop going; my mother's a widow and takes in washing, but it only just covers the rent. Without me and my brothers all working, we'd have nought to eat. I told the wagon-men about him, but when they look he's gone." Tears welled up in his eyes. "He won't leave me be. I fear he'll kill me."

Paix put his hand on the boy's. "We'll get the artist so we can draw a portrait of the man. We'll catch him."

The boy visibly relaxed, sniffled. "I'm sorry, sir. I didn't know where else to turn."

"You did well," Paix said. Then he turned to C.K.. "I confess I don't understand what this has to do with our investigations."

C.K. shifted in his chair. "Master Rivers, pray tell the Constable what you told me. About the lady."

Stephen sniffled. "I went by the poorhouse last Tuesday and there was a big crowd. Lots of rich ladies. One gave me a sandwich and asked about a missing boy. David Bryce."

A shock went through him. "You're sure that's the name."

Stephen nodded, then wiped his eyes with his sleeve. "She

said she'd see me the next day. I went to meet her and she gave me money to go look for him. A whole half dollar!" He seemed astonished at the amount. "I tried to give it to my mother, but she wants me to give it back. She thinks I got tangled in something bad, that's why the man follows me."

This gave Paix some concern. How would a "rich lady" even know about a boy missing on 2nd Street, much less by name? "Did the lady give her name?"

The boy glanced away. "Don't want to squeal, sir. She meant me no harm."

C.K. put his elbows on the table. "Now we're helping you from the man who's following. You want our help, you tell us about the lady."

Stephen looked back and forth at us, then his shoulders sagged. "She said her name was Eunice Ogier. That's all I know."

"What did she look like?"

"Brown hair. Old, like twenty or thirty."

"What was she wearing?"

Stephen shrugged. "Fancy clothes. Wore mourning the second time."

Paix considered this. A young rich woman. What was her interest in David's case? And who was following Stephen? "What happened there to your hand?" It looked well-healed, with a faint white scar.

Stephen hung his head. "Had a good job once. Five cents a day at the mill. A man's job, but they was short and I came on the right day for it. But I got my finger caught in the machine. They let me go after that, said a nine-fingered boy was bad for morale. Five cents a day!" His eyes filled with tears. "We could have moved up. I had everything and I ruined it." He put his head in his hands. "Not only do I make less now, we have to pay the surgeon."

C.K. leaned forward. "Still?"

Stephen nodded.

C.K. rose. "Don't fret, son; I'll talk with this surgeon." He gestured to Paix. "Bring this young man to the artist."

Paix got Stephen settled beside the artist, then went to find C.K., who was writing up a warrant. "I've heard stories like this before," C.K. muttered. "Damn surgeon spends twenty minutes on a stitch-up job, doubles the rate for those he knows can't pay, then charges interest until they do. The widow'll be paying him until she dies. It's a swindle, pure and simple." He glanced at Paix. "You find out about this event. I'll take care of this."

"What's going to happen to the boy?"

"Once the artist's done with the portrait, we'll see who it is, and go from there."

Paix got a wagon from the yard. When they got to the poorhouse, Paix asked the wagon driver to wait, then went inside.

A middle-aged woman wearing the traditional dark green robe and headscarf of the Dealers greeted him. "How may I help, Constable?"

Paix bowed low. "Blessed Lady, I'm here for information on your event last Tuesday."

She went to a ledger, opened it. "The event was held by Mrs. Jacqueline Spadros."

Spadros. "Were there any other events here that day?"

"No, Constable, none this month but hers so far."

"And do you know what ladies accompanied her?"

"You'd have to ask Mrs. Spadros that. We had nothing to do with it. More an event for the paper, in my view: they never once came inside."

"I see. Thank you for seeing me." He bowed and left.

On the way back to the station, Paix felt a sense of doom. The Spadros Family and a missing little boy.

Not again. He remembered the small crumpled body of the boy who'd stolen from them. That had all but ruined him — not only had he lost his shield, he'd had nightmares for years after.

When Paix told C.K. what he'd learned, C.K. got quiet for a while. "Come see what the artist drew."

C.K. went to his desk, opened a folder. "Looks a bit like a Spadros Associate I've seen once or twice before." He pursed his lips in thought. "Wait here."

Paix leaned on the desk. A rich young woman with the Spadros Family asking about a missing outsider boy in the slums. A Spadros Associate following a young man who searched for the boy. Another young man — the boy's brother — dead.

No, he thought. Not just Herbert. Caddy Arrenegada was dead too, by the same hand.

What connected Caddy Arrenegada with Herbert Bryce?

C.K. strode up. "The Commander wants to see you."

Commander Green sat on the edge of his desk when Paix walked in. "Come on in, sit down." He got up and walked around the desk to take his own seat as well.

Paix felt odd sitting in the Commander's presence.

"I know how you feel about the Spadros Family," the Commander said. "But I need answers, and I need them today. Kanhu's drunk already, so you have the job.

"Now, I want you to be careful and discreet at this, Hanger. We'll go over everything; just do and say exactly what I tell you to and you should be out of there in no time."

Paix peered at him, confused. "What is it you want me to do?"

Commander Green's head drew back a bit in surprise. "Why, go talk with Mrs. Spadros and find out which of her ladies spoke with that boy."

15

It was midday by the time Paix arrived at Spadros Manor. The ride there left him awed at the ever- increasing grandeur of the homes, the fineness of the roads, the ease in the faces of those they passed.

"Wait here," he told the driver, and went to the door.

The butler, a man in his fifties, answered the door. "Mrs. Spadros is at her dress-maker's, but should be home momentarily." He gestured for Paix to follow, and led him to a parlor close by. "You're not to sit in the Lady's presence," he said, then left.

Paix stood facing the room as the door shut behind him. The room — this one room — was twice the size of his parents' entire home. The walls, paneled white. The floor, gray tile. The furnishings, white, with cushions in pale blue. Fine paintings hung on the walls, fresh plants grew in pots. All was spotless, rich, dazzling.

He felt grateful not to have brought Briscola here. This place felt like a trap.

The door opened. The butler said, "Mrs. Jacqueline Spadros."

So soon? From what the Commander had said, Paix expected a long wait while the visit was cleared with the woman's husband.

A young woman came in. She wore a deep green dress and hat with a veil, which seemed odd. Why did she wear her hat — and veil — indoors?

She said, "May I help you?"

"Yes, mum. I am investigating a case of a missing child, and would like to ask some questions."

She was quite pretty — light brown skin, curls of a reddish brown, fine form — yet something unexpected lay in her deep blue eyes. Fear? "I am at a loss." She sat, gesturing for Paix to sit. "Anything I can do to help, I am glad to."

Paix felt torn. He'd been told not to sit, yet feared causing offense. So he sat. But he didn't let down his guard, not here. "Are you familiar with a woman by the name of Eunice Ogier?"

"Should I be?"

Paix couldn't shake the feeling something wasn't right. "I have in custody a boy who says this woman Eunice Ogier asked him about the missing boy by name. He also says this woman was there at the same time," which meant Mrs. Spadros must have seen her, even briefly. "'A rich woman,' he says, gave food to the poor. The only group there on the day he mentioned was yours.

"He stated she gave him food as well. I thought she might have been one of your ladies. We would like to learn what she knows of the matter."

Mrs Spadros shook her head. "I know of no living woman by that name. I'm sorry. Could she be a relative?"

Paix shook his head, disheartened. This was a dead end. "The boy's mother is his only living family." He rose. "I'm sorry to have bothered you, mum."

She rose as well. "I wish you the best of success."

"Thank you, mum."

As he turned towards the door, he saw a tiny motion. So someone had watched them, listened.

None of this felt right. Although Mrs. Spadros seemed outwardly fine, he felt she hid something. That she knew more about this than she let on.

I know of no living woman by that name.

What an odd way to answer a simple question, Paix thought. He stared out of the carriage window. Everything about the visit felt odd.

When he returned to the station, the desk clerk told him the Commander wanted to see him at once. So Paix went back up the two flights of stairs to the Commander's office.

The Commander bounded from his chair when Paix entered. "Did all go well?"

Paix stood in the doorway, puzzled. Did it? "She knows

something, or suspects," he said. Then he felt weary. "But of course, she told me nothing."

Commander Green smiled to himself and sat. "Sit down, Hanger. Tell me everything."

So Paix did, slowly, and with hesitation. "I had the distinct feeling she hid something. The whole event was quite odd."

"Well, it sounds as if you did your best. Good work." He leaned back in his chair. "So what's your next play?"

"I'd like to investigate this Eunice Ogier. If she truly wasn't with Mrs. Spadros, then perhaps she used the event as cover to contact the boy."

"Interesting idea," the Commander said. "Very well, find all you can about the woman and report back to me."

"To you, sir? I thought I was reporting to Detective Senior Constable Kanhu."

"You may certainly tell him of your findings, Constable, but I want to know first. Understand?"

Paix felt something wasn't right here as well. "Yes, Commander."

Paix returned to his desk to write his report.

I know of no living woman by that name.

Who could Eunice Ogier be? And how did she know about David's disappearance?

Paix got up to file his reports. On the way, C.K. stopped him. "I remembered who this man," he brandished the drawing, "reminded me of. They call him Crab." C.K. rubbed his eyes. "A Spadros Associate. He's been picked up several times for following people." He pulled a photo of a young man from his pocket; the portraits did look similar. "Never charged with killing anyone, though."

"What do we know about him?"

"Lives over on 25th in a boarding-house. Two roommates. All three just recently made Associate." He fished in his pocket again, came out with a scrap of paper. "Here's the address. Bring him in."

"Be happy to," Paix said.

But when he got to the address, no one at the boarding-house had seen any of the men in weeks. The housekeeper was evidently annoyed. "They don't show up with their rent, I'll have them in the street. Those three are altogether too chummy with each other for my liking."

"Any family or friends that you know of?"

"One said his parents were on 7th, but I don't know where."

* * *

Paix had the carriage bring him by the beat station. "Any news on my men?"

"No."

So he walked along Snow looking for them. He eventually caught up to them at 5th and Snow as they were walking back to the beat station.

"You didn't need to come worry after us," Briscola said. "We had a couple deaders and a fight, but we took care of it." He glanced at Lightner. "Right?"

Lightner nodded.

"Well, then," Paix said, surprised, "good job."

Briscola stopped then. "So what's going on with the boy?"

Paix told them about the street gang boy Stephen Rivers who'd been followed, and the woman Eunice Ogier who seemed to know about the case.

Briscola clapped his hand to his forehead. "Unbelievable."

"And get this," Paix said, "Detective Senior Constable Kanhu thinks the man following the boy is a Spadros man."

"Oh," Briscola said, dismayed. "So this woman sneaks into the event, talks to the boy, then maybe this guy follows him to see what he knows?" He paced about a bit. "You think this Spadros man is the one taking the kids? Murdering them?"

"I don't know," Paix said. "But whoever it was frightened the kid near to death. The Commander told me to bring the Associate in, but no one's seen the man in weeks." He started towards the wagons, and the other two followed. "Lightner, you're sure getting an education. How long are you with us?"

"Another week, sir. Constable. And my buddies are fair jealous, to be sure. One hasn't left the station the whole month."

Paix grinned. "We'll put in a good word for you."

"Much obliged, s— Constable."

Paix sat back during the trip back to the station and listened to the two younger men banter about their day. It was good to see them finally working together.

He'd type up a letter of recommendation for the Trainee and have Briscola sign it first. That way, there'd be someone else other than the Pariah of Precinct 1 recommending the kid.

Paix sat forward. "Lightner, you been doing reports?"

"Yes, sir."

Paix smiled. He used to make the same mistake when he was a Trainee. "Constable."

"Yes, Constable. Sorry, Constable."

"Well, I want one for today on my desk in the morning. All you did. You'll be a Probationary soon — you'll need the practice."

"Yes — Constable."

Lightner would turn out well. Hopefully better than we did, Paix thought.

C.K. and Jake, him and Sheinwold. A bunch of tired, aging men trying to survive in a place that'd already about ground them to dust.

Would he survive to spend his pension? He wasn't sure.

Reina would say he was moping, and perhaps he was.

The carriage arrived at the station, and they got out. Lightner bounded inside, but Briscola hung back. "So what's next?"

"I have reports to write, same as you."

"Then what?"

"I'll have better luck at the Backdoor than knocking on every front door on 7th. Mr. Howell," Paix almost called him their old name, "Eighty–Eight", but Briscola wouldn't understand, "probably knows where he's gone."

"You want some backup?"

Paix considered this. "Sure. Why not?"

* * *

Before they left the station, Paix put a background check request on this Eunice Ogier. The office man surprised him by handing him the report, already done. "The Commander asked for it, so I went to City Hall myself."

"Very good," Paix said. Mrs. Spadros was right: the only woman ever registered as Eunice Ogier was a maid at the Spadros Country House who died eight years ago at the age of 97.

Someone was using her name as an alias.

Paix turned to Briscola. "Come on, it's getting late."

They signed out a driver and carriage to take them to the Backdoor Saloon, and while on the way, Paix thought about this woman calling herself Eunice Ogier. It was an uncommon name, unlikely to be confused with someone else. Certainly a dead woman didn't need the name anymore, and no one would suspect the real Eunice Ogier lay buried in the countryside.

Paix liked Briscola's theory on the surface, but when you dug deeper it slid away like sand. A rich woman — or in any case, pretending to be rich, there was always that. Helping a runaway family newly arrived in the slums. With a Spadros man following a boy who talked to her? And why the Red Dog stamp?

Paix wished he had spoken to Stephen Rivers about how far he'd gotten in searching for David Bryce. But the boy was so terrified he probably wouldn't be able to tell them much.

Stephen hadn't been the one who put the mark on that alley wall, or he surely would have said so when this Miss Ogier asked about David. Someone else was involved, too.

"Constable Hanger?"

Briscola's words brought Paix out of his reverie. "Yes?"

"Are you well?"

"I was simply thinking that we may be dealing with two groups here."

Briscola shook his head a bit. "Two?"

"Just consider it. How high from the ground was that Red Dogs mark?"

Briscola shrugged. "Perhaps waist high. A bit less."

"But we're talking about children eight to fifteen. Wouldn't they have put the mark higher?" Paix put his hands out at chest level as if holding a stamp. "When you stamp something, you have to press it, like so, with your body behind it. Especially if it were onto a rough wall."

"So we're either talking about smaller children —"

"In which case, the mark would be less distinct. They're smaller, and have less force behind them —"

"Or ...." Briscola frowned slightly.

"Or this is someone who'd very much like us to **believe** children did this. Someone who crouched."

The light dawned in Briscola's face. "An adult. The strangler?"

"That we don't know. We can only hope David didn't meet that fate. But it does raise the question of why Stephen Rivers is being followed."

"You think he saw something he shouldn't."

"Yes," Paix said, "perhaps something he doesn't even know he saw." He pondered this a moment. "Criminals often become filled with paranoia. The guilt of their crime weighs on them to the point they become convinced everyone knows of it. This young man had no powers of observation, but this villain doesn't know that. He was there, he saw something — or the man imagines he saw something — and a young man becomes a danger."

"So what happens to him?"

"I expect Detective Senior Constable Kanhu will either send Stephen Rivers home with an officer to watch his door, or keep him there at the station overnight. He'll be safe enough."

* * *

When they arrived at the Backdoor Saloon, quite a few more people were there, and cigar smoke filled the room. Paix asked for Howell and was shown back.

Eight Howell sat behind his desk with a drink in his hand. "What can I do for you, Constables?" He gestured to the two chairs in front of the desk. "By all means, sit."

After they sat, Paix said, "Remember the kid I asked about?"

"Yeah, sure, I do."

"We need to talk with Crab. We think he may have seen him."

Howell leaned his elbows on the desk. "Now that's going to be difficult."

"Why?"

"Because no one's seen him. We got the whole quadrant out

looking for the man."

Paix felt taken aback. "He's missing too?"

"Three weeks now," Howell said. "Last anyone's seen him was New Year's Day."

"Well, that's odd," Briscola said, "because there's a boy at the station says they saw him today."

Howell gaped at them. "Are you certain?"

"No," Paix said. "We have a drawing that resembles him, that's all. The boy came in frightened and told us a man'd been following him."

"I see." Howell hesitated a moment. "Well, if you do find him, let me know."

* * *

The next morning, the east beat overnight had found one of Caddy's missing friends, also strangled. C.K. and the detective assigned to that case went into a huddle after the pre-shift briefing, so Paix, Briscola, and Lightner went on their beat.

When the three sat at luncheon, C.K. hurried up to them. "Found you," he panted.

Paix hadn't seen C.K. rushing about like that in years. "What's happened? Here, sit down."

C.K. plopped onto a chair, out of breath. "The handmarks are identical, Hanger. Identical."

Lightner blinked. "What handmarks?"

Paix waved him away. "Quiet." He leaned forward. "So all three boys, the same?"

"All three." C.K. took out a handkerchief and wiped his face. "The first in Diamond, but the other two right here in Spadros, within a few blocks of each other." He got excited. "You know what that means?"

Paix smiled, remembering his detective training. "We know where he lives. Or close to it."

Briscola said, "So where does he live?"

"East side, somewhere around the mid 20's."

Paix sighed. "Crab."

"Does add more evidence to our suspicions."

Paix leaned back. *Why put the other boy in Diamond?*

Then Paix told C.K. his thoughts about the stamp. "This fellow is crafty. He put Herbert Bryce in Diamond to separate that crime from the other two. He's trying to throw us off." That raised another question. "Why is Herbert Bryce different from Caddy and his friend?"

"They live in different areas," C.K. said. "Herbert was an outsider. Other than that, I can't see why he'd bother —"

"Wait," Paix said. "How did he get the body to Diamond in the first place? Herbert Bryce was as tall as Briscola here. He didn't just say 'la-dee-dah, Master Bryce, let's go to Diamond so I can kill you' —"

Briscola snickered.

"— so he had to have help. And a carriage."

"Which means a driver," C.K. said. "How many are involved in this? It's uncommon for a multiple murderer to have a team!"

"We're talking of at least two men," Paix said. "One wealthy enough to own a carriage but not so high they'd balk at driving it."

Paix and C.K. locked eyes. *Or they might steal it.* The crime which a boy had been caught for, so many years ago, a boy the Spadros Family murdered.

Detective Constable Paix Hanger, Detective Constable Jake Bower, and an Officer Trainee named Cartas Kanhu.

The case that about ended me. Paix shook his head to drive away the memories. "They had to cross the bridge to Diamond. We have the artist's drawing. We can start there."

* * *

Paix sent a surly Briscola (who wanted to come too) and a pensive Lightner to finish the beat patrol, telling them he'd catch up to them later. He and C.K. got into one of the police carriages patrolling the Promenade and went to the bridge to Diamond.

C.K. had made a KASLOF flyer with the drawing, handing one to the guards on both sides of the bridge. None of them had seen a man who looked anything like the description. But they promised to post the flyer and report back.

The carriage returned to the Precinct 1 station. "Decent

chaps," C.K. said, tossing his coat over the back of his chair. "Hell of a job, standing there all day telling uppers whether they're allowed past or not."

Paix chuckled. "I'd say I liked the idea —"

"Except for the part about dealing with the uppers."

Who were mostly in one Family or another. "You're right, I wouldn't last long." *I'd probably say something wrong and end up without a job. Especially if I saw a Spadros thug shoving his weight around.* "By the way, whatever happened to that boy?"

"Sent him home with an officer. Gave him a dime and told him to stay in until we get this sorted."

Paix felt relieved. "Good."

"By the way," C.K. said. "The Old Man wants you to help me out on Saturday."

"I suppose," Paix said, "so long as I get paid."

C.K. chuckled at that.

A messenger boy ran into the station. "Officers need assistance at the Pocket Pair!"

"I better go," Paix said. "Let me know what happens."

"Have fun," C.K. said, peering at his stacks of folders.

Paix ran outside just in time to hop on the wagon's running board with the rest as it started off, clinging to the upper bar as the wagon trundled along.

The Pocket Pair was a big rowdy saloon near 17th and Broadway. A fight there wasn't that unusual; a fight at this time of day was.

"Gang brawl, I reckon," the Probationary next to him said.

Stating the obvious. But in broad daylight?

As they pulled up to the saloon, the fight spilled out into the street, at least fifty men using fists, chairs, bottles, whatever they might find. A man standing across the street smoking left the lampost he'd been leaning on and began walking off.

"Hanger," one of the east beat guys said, "gonna help or not?"

Paix snapped his head around. "Sure." He jogged over and began pulling men off of each other as the chain wagons and ambulances arrived.

He never did meet up with Briscola and Lightner; by the time the chain wagon got to the station, they got the men booked, in their cells, it was well dark.

Paix slumped in his chair without even taking off his jacket.

"Hell," C.K. said, still where Paix left him several hours before, "you look as bad as I feel."

I still have reports, and the wagon to the island has left, he thought wearily. He could find a cot in the barracks for an hour or two, do these later.

No, he thought. Reina would surely worry. And if he lay down, he was likely to sleep all night. He struggled to his feet, hung his jacket over the chair, and sat back down to type. If he didn't do these reports now, he never would find the time.

Ten years to go. "I'm getting too old for this," Paix mumbled.

* * *

By the time Paix got home, it was after ten. Reina came to meet him in her robe. "Are you well?" She touched a tender spot below his eye. "You're hurt."

"Bar brawl," Paix said, stripping off his uniform. "A big one. Took hours to get everyone tucked in."

Reina snorted in amusement. "Let me chip some ice for that." She scraped frozen snow off the windowsill with a knife, which she tied up in a cloth and handed to him.

Paix put on some clean clothes and collapsed into a chair. He pressed the ice bag on his cheek, which throbbed. "There must be an easier way to make a living." He sighed. "And they want me working on Saturday."

"My poor dear." She put his feet on a chair, sat on the bed beside him.

"At least some Family didn't collect their men before we even finished the reports, like last time."

"There is that."

Paix surveyed her. Reina's face held more color, and she sat straighter. But a sadness hung on her. "Something's happened."

"Heap Tableau spent the entire day sniping at me. Little comments here and there about us, how we lived together, how I should be back home with my husband. Nothing I could call him out on, but ...."

"I know. He did the same at the tent meeting. I don't know why he feels how we live is his concern." He placed his hand on hers. "I'm sorry he upset you."

Reina sighed. "I'm grateful for what they've done to help me, but I don't know how much longer I can continue like this. It's been going on for a while, but today was the worst. And Lane sits like nothing is happening."

"Are there other knitted shops which might want you to do their spinning?"

Reina nodded her head slowly, eyes downcast. "I'll walk about tomorrow and see. Ask about their rates."

"I'm so sorry it's come to this." Paix smoothed her hair. "Would it help if I spoke with him again?"

"I don't think it would," she said, "and it might make him worse. He's determined that you're taking advantage; half the time, his mutterings are about you. I fear it might come to blows should you approach him."

He's made her life even harder — because of me. "You take the west side there. If I can, I'll go by after work and search the north." He squeezed her hand. "Never fear; somehow, we'll find a way through this."

* * *

Fortunately, the next day's patrol was quiet. Paix wanted to speak with Pattsz about the charity event, but he arrived as they were on their way to patrol, and by the time he returned to the station, the Lead Constable had already left.

After the wagon arrived at the Market Center police station, Paix asked the driver if he might drop him at the north-east end of the Plaza.

"You think I'm a taxi-carriage? Once I arrive here, I'm off duty, and I've got the care of these horses and the wagon before I leave. Do your shopping on your own time, Constable, not mine."

So Paix broke down and paid the penny for a taxi to the other side of the island. Shoes were more expensive than taxis, and foot doctors more expensive still.

Paix spoke with a few knitted goods sellers. Some bought from others and simply resold, others had plenty of spinners already. One woman perked up when he mentioned Lane's shop. "I've been there; I like to spy out the competition. Fine work she does, and her husband too."

"Well, my sister is inquiring about work as a spinner. How much do you pay?"

"Three cents a hundred-yard skein is the going rate. Natural or dyed?"

Three cents? For all that work? But he collected himself. "She's only ever done natural, but she's interested in learning to dye."

"I could go up to four cents a skein dyed, if it's well-spun."

Paix took a card, promising to give it to his "sister". As it turned out, this would be the best offer of the lot.

The sky was almost dark when he entered his building. He trudged up the four flights and down the long hallway, knocked, then used the key. Two women sat there, turning towards him as he entered.

Reina's face was pale.

"Hello, Paix," Lane said.

16

At first, Paix just stood there, mouth open. Then he recovered, closed the door. "What a surprise."

Lane let out a short laugh. "I had to see this for myself. It's exactly as I pictured."

"Lane's here as a friend," Reina said. "Come, change your clothes, then we can talk."

Paix took everything into their tiny toilet room next to the bed and changed, mind racing.

Why was Lane here? Why visit now? What would she tell Heap? Things were bad enough for Reina already.

Settle yourself, Paix thought. *Reina said Lane came as a friend.*

He took a deep breath, let it out, and emerged. The two women sat eating dinner as if all were perfectly normal.

Reina glanced up. "I made a plate for you. Come, sit down, my love. All will be well."

Paix sat warily on the edge of the bed. "To what do we owe this honor?"

Lane leaned forward. "I don't want Reina to leave."

This surprised him. "Then why are you here?"

"Paix," Reina said, "hear her out."

Paix leaned back, crossed his arms. "I'm listening."

Lane glanced at Reina. "We had a long talk. About everything. And — and I need her to stay." She sighed, peering at her plate. "It's been twenty years since I joined the Bridgers. Reina tells me you know now why I did it."

Paix shrugged. "Reina guessed."

"Well, it's true. I gained a husband, but that's about all. Bridger women — including my own children — speak of nothing else but their home and tenets. Anyone not in the Bridgers shuns me when they learn my affiliation." She smiled to herself. "It's been good to have someone to talk to."

She must feel as out of place as I do. Filled with compassion, he reached across the table and squeezed his cousin's hand.

When she looked up at him, tears lay in her eyes.

So we have an ally. "What will you do?"

"I'm here investigating the matter." Lane smiled, and sniffled, and reached for her handkerchief. "I'll go home, and Heap and I will argue. I'll tell him all is proper, because you have two rooms, and Reina has a maid who shares her room. I'll tell him you're helping Reina out of a bad situation with her husband. I'll tell him he's a filthy-minded fool, and that we almost lost Reina's help because of his bullying." She grinned at Reina. "After a day or two of awkward apology, he'll never say another word about it." She pulled a thin pair of knitting needles out of her oversized purse and began casting on some fine white thread.

Paix felt a great weight fall from his shoulders. "I've misjudged you. I'm sorry."

She stopped then, and gave him a warm smile. "All is forgiven." She glanced around. "Look at this place. You still have the coverlet I made." She began to knit. "Our two weeks of rebellion seems so long ago."

At that, Paix chuckled. "Is that what it was?"

"It was," Lane said. "The good kind, that leads to freedom."

* * *

When Paix woke, Reina was sitting up in bed. "I had the strangest dream. Lane wore one of those Memory Girl coats, the red ones, and she went back and forth bringing messages to Heap from us."

"Was she a child?"

"No," Reina said, "the age she is now. But it didn't seem odd." She fell silent for a while, then said, "No one ever questions a dream when they're in it."

For some reason, this stuck with Paix all the way to the station. Before the briefing, Paix asked Lead Constable Pattsz about the charity event. "Didn't see anything unusual," Pattsz said.

After the pre-shift briefing, C.K. pulled Paix aside. "Tell your men to go on. I've got something to show you."

When Paix entered the tiny interrogation room, a man sat handcuffed to the chair.

The man was young, perhaps twenty. Thinning brown hair, hazel eyes. "Why do you have me here? I've done nothing wrong."

C.K. put the drawing in front of him. "Look familiar?"

The man flinched when he saw it. "Could be anyone."

"We've had a complaint of following, and this is the portrait the artist got. Looks an awful lot like you."

"I've been following no one," the man said. "And I'll not be bullied into confession. My lads will get me from here, you'll see."

Paix frowned. "Aren't you Crab? Your friends are all looking for you."

"They found me," Crab said. "I was with them when your lads caught me."

C.K. turned aside. "Raid on the Pocket Pair last night. One of the Constables recalled the KASLOF and brought him in late last night with the rest."

"They find anything?"

"Just some 'working girls' in the quadrant without papers."

Paix grunted. This happened from time to time. Back to the Pot they'd go, and they'd fine the owner. He said to Crab, "Your housekeeper says you've been gone three weeks. Where've you been all this time?"

Crab glanced away. "Don't wish to speak of it."

Paix sat across from him. "Now look. We have a complaint. We have a drawing of you. You've been picked up three times before for following. And you can't give us your whereabouts. Do I need to have a lineup? Or will you just tell us why you're following and what you want from him?"

Crab's eyes narrowed. "Who made the complaint?"

"You know we can't say that. The boy's frightened enough."

At the word "boy," Crab relaxed. "Well, it warn't me. I've followed no boy, sir. You've got the wrong man."

This last bit seemed to ring true.

C.K.'s face darkened, and he leaned both fists on the table.

"Listen here, you. We're hunting a murderer —"

Crab paled.

"— and we know he's got an accomplice. These are boys he's murdering, sir, and another's missing."

At the word "missing", Crab flinched.

"Now you can tell me what you know of this, or I'll tell every thug in the city you're a stool pigeon on my payroll."

C.K.'s threat seemed to unnerve the man. "But I don't know nothing about no murder! I swear on the Deck, I had nothing to do with mur —" At that, his face fell, and he put his forehead on the table's edge, sobbing.

He's barely more than a boy, and he's gotten into trouble. "Look," Paix said, "we don't want to go hard on you. We just want to find this murderer before he kills anyone else."

"I know," Crab said, his forehead still on the table. "Might you loose my hands so I can get my kerchief?"

C.K. undid his handcuffs. Crab took out a brown kerchief and wiped his nose. Paix said, "Now what's upsetting you so?"

"I can't say it all," Crab said, not looking at them. "But I've had friends killed on my account." At this he hesitated a long time. "Recently."

"Is that why you've been away?"

Crab nodded, eyes downcast.

"Did you go away on a mourning trip, or were you taken?"

Crab's eyes filled with tears. "T–taken."

Paix and C.K. exchanged a glance. Crab hadn't looked at the portrait since it'd first been brought out. Paix said, "Is this the man who took you?"

Crab didn't move. "Don't know."

Paix got up, gestured for C.K. to follow. Once they'd stepped out of the room and closed the door, Paix said, "Do you think this man escaped him? The murderer."

"No," C.K. said. "I think this is an act."

Paix stared at him, appalled. "You do?"

"Yes, I do." He locked the door. "I'm going to send for Stephen Rivers and put this man in a lineup. We'll see then, won't we?"

Since Paix wasn't needed, he caught up with Briscola and Lightner. He found them taking the man with the shotgun to a waiting chain wagon, his wife wailing on the steps behind him.

Paix felt astonished. "What happened here?"

"He came out and threatened me with the damn shotgun is what happened," Briscola said. "So I took it from him." He turned to the constable who'd arrived at their whistle. "Charge him with threatening an officer, assault with a deadly weapon," he glanced at the man's wife, who sported a black eye, "and wife-beating."

"With pleasure," the constable said.

"Well done," Paix said. "Make sure —"

"— to take notes," Briscola said. "I know."

"You'll need them when you appear in court."

Briscola paled. "I have to go to court?"

"You're the arresting officer."

"Oh." This seemed to cause him dismay.

Paix laughed, clapping him on the shoulder. "Don't worry. If you make good notes and type up a complete report, you can just read it when you appear. Easy peasy."

Lightner stood gaping. "Weren't you afraid of the gun?"

Briscola said, "It's the man who's dangerous, my Pa used to say, not the gun. And that man's a bully, nothing more. When we went against him in strength, he folded."

Briscola evidently had better cards than Paix thought. "Well," Paix said, holding out a hand, "I'm pleased with you both. How about after you write your reports, we go to luncheon? I'll buy your meals."

They shook hands, both younger men standing taller as they did so.

Is this what it feels like to be a father? For an instant, Paix felt that perhaps it was.

* * *

When they returned to the station, C.K. sat behind his desk, drinking from a flask in full view of everyone. Paix went up to him. "What the hell are you doing? You can't drink in here!"

C.K. snorted. "You know, Hanger, I think getting fired might be the best thing for me."

"What do you mean?"

"I mean," C.K. said, as if speaking to a child, "that not two hours after you left, Sawbuck was here, and got Crab out."

Paix felt horrified. "No."

"Yes. And what's even worse? Stephen Rivers is gone."

"What?"

"The officer I sent says his mother hasn't seen him since yesterday. He gave her the money, stayed in a few days, then she turns around and he's gone."

"Why didn't she call a messenger? Put in a report?"

"I went there myself. She said that she didn't the have money for police bribes. She and her other sons have been out looking for him themselves."

"This is bad," Paix said. "We have to find that boy. He's the only real lead we have."

"I got his portrait, requested a KASLOF for him," C.K. said. "But as scared as he was, he could have gone anywhere."

He can't have gotten far. Stephen Rivers had no money, and would be hiding everywhere he went.

Child ... messenger ... the Memory Boy ....

"Hanger? What is it?"

Paix put up his hand. "One moment."

He rushed out to the messenger booth, ignoring the strange looks Briscola, Lightner, and C.K. were giving him, and found a group of the boys sitting there. "Have you ever taken a message from or sent one to a woman named Eunice Ogier?"

Most of them shook their heads, but one, a round-faced boy of ten with coiled black hair and very dark skin, considered the matter. "I did, sir, over a year ago. I remember it because they sent me in the carriage, all the way to the country."

"Really? What quadrant?"

"Spadros. It was from Spadros Manor to the Spadros Country House. A grand place it was, sir, to be sure."

"Did they have a reply?"

"No, sir, they said they'd call if they needed to send one." He beamed then. "But they tipped very well."

"Thank you, you may put in a duty bill at the desk inside."

The boy's face said "oh!" He ran in, the rest cheering for him.

Paix went inside more slowly. He'd have to talk to the Commander about this.

***

Commander Green looked up from his desk. "Kanhu is in a panic about our one lead gone missing and you want to joy-ride to the Spadros Country House?"

"We have another lead. This woman Eunice Ogier has sent messages there. Someone must know her. If we can find her —"

"Then what? Didn't you say she was looking for David Bryce too? She doesn't know any more than we do."

"But what if she does? Don't you see? The family must trust her if they've sent her to look for him. Maybe they've told her something they kept back from us. But there's another matter. What if she's with the kidnappers, trying to see what people know of it?"

"Hanger —"

"We have to at least talk to her, or we'll never know."

"You're drawing thin here, Constable. To question the Spadros Country House on the word of a messenger? And how will you find who she sent the mail to? Ask everyone there? The place must have near a hundred workers."

"If that's what it takes, I'm prepared to do it. And we must do it now. These scoundrels have killed anyone remotely involved with this case, and now, as you say, Stephen Rivers is gone. What if they target Miss Ogier? If she's taken it upon herself to search for the boy it's vital we find her before they do."

The Commander sighed. "Very well, Hanger. Go." He pulled out a quarter page form, made a few notes, signed it, handed it over. "Show this to the driver."

Permission to travel to the countryside. "Thank you, Commander."

After he bought his men their luncheon, Paix set off. It was a long ride to the Country House, past rolling fields, grazing sheep and cattle. Trees stood in the distance past carriage windows shut against the cold. The sun hung low in the sky before he reached the Country House.

This place appeared more a manor than the mansion he'd visited earlier. Set far back from the road, sheep grazed the expanse in front of a tall, wide, white building with grand columns. Men in Spadros livery stood on either side of the roofed entry, and a well-dressed butler came to greet them.

"Eunice Ogier, you say? I've not heard that name in some time." The butler, a man in his later sixties, perused a series of thick ledgers. "Ah, here. Yes, a letter came to our Miss Call. Shall I have you brought to her?"

Paix thought she'd be called up, but he said, "Certainly, sir."

"Very good." The man pulled a bell-cord, and presently a footman strode up. "Take the Constable to Miss Call's cottage."

Paix followed the tall young man through a long hallway which ran along the front of the Country House and through a side door which led to a packed dirt path. This path ran along past stables, barns, and gardens, before opening onto a row of cottages. At the fourteenth one on the left, the footman knocked, and a young woman wearing a blue dress with a white apron and headscarf opened the door. "Yes?"

"Constable here for Miss Call."

"Right this way." She led Paix to a side room: a tiny parlor. There sat an ancient woman taking tea. The woman looked up when they arrived; her eyes were clouded with blindness white.

The younger woman said, "Miss Call, you have a visitor."

Miss Call's face turned joyous. "Oh, I'm so grateful. My dear little Jacqui, is it you?"

"I'm Constable Paix Hanger from Precinct 1 downtown. Might we have a word in private?"

"Constable?" She laughed. "Now what sort of trouble might I get into at my age?"

"You're not in trouble, Miss Call. I merely have questions for you. I'm investigating a series of murders —"

"Gracious me!"

"And I've heard you received mail from someone connected to the case."

"Oh, very well. Henny, my dear, go on. I'll call when we're done here. Constable, would you care for some tea?"

"Yes, of course." He sat; Henny poured his tea then closed the door behind her.

"Henny's such a dear girl, comes in to fix my meals, run my bath, give me my tonics. Here eight-twelve-four-eight, like clockwork. You'd think I was a grand lady! Don't know what I'd do without her."

He took a sip, added cream. "Do you know a woman named Eunice Ogier?"

A sly smile crossed her face. "I do! Many years now."

"How is it that you know her?"

"Since she was a small girl."

"Was she a maid here?"

"Oh, no. A visitor. We've known each other for years. I went to the city once and we met there and formed a friendship. She visits when she can, comes and goes as she pleases."

"When did you last see her?"

"Oh, it's been some time since I've **seen** anyone. My eyes and all. They say there's nothing can be done." She seemed sad at that. "And I did so love to read."

"I'm very sorry to hear that." He paused, not quite sure where to begin. "I'm told you correspond."

"We do, here and there."

"Do you have any of her letters?"

"What good would saved letters be to a blind woman?" She let out a short laugh, then shook her head.

Something about the way she said this made him uneasy. "I understand. But it's vital we contact Miss Ogier. She may be in serious danger. Do you have an address for her?"

Her eyes, though blind, darted up and to the side, and her shoulders tensed a bit. "Not as yet, sir."

"As yet?"

She straightened, and her smile became too bright. "Why, she's moved. Left the city, she did. I'm sorry I can't be of more help, but as I said, she's not contacted me yet with an address. Here, have a bit of cake."

"Thank you, I believe I will," Paix said, taking a thin piece of spongecake. "When did she leave the city?"

"I can't say exactly, Constable. These young girls flit about so. Like sparrows, they do."

The cake was excellent, as was the tea. "You say she left for good? Or might she return?"

"Oh, no. She got a definite offer. And before you ask, I don't know where or with who or nothing else." She gave a sharp nod, mouth pursed, the sort given to a small boy who begged for treats past his bedtime. "And that's all I have to say about it."

"Well, you've been most helpful," he said, not feeling at all so. He drained his teacup and rose. "Good evening to you. I appreciate your hospitality."

She blushed. "Why, it's nothing, Constable. I'm grateful to the Spadros Family for their care. Eighty-seven years I've been in service. Worked my way to Mistress of Kitchens, I did, and I've been given everything I need, as if one of their very own!"

Paix smiled, feeling touched, yet not knowing why. "I'm pleased to hear it. Thank you for seeing me, Miss Call."

"You be safe, sir. And I hope you catch your murderer."

"Thank you." He went to the door, leaving her sitting there, a bemused smile on her face.

* * *

After the long trip back to the city, Paix typed out a warrant application, went to Commander Green and told him all which had happened. "The woman knows more than she's letting on, Commander." When he'd gotten out of the carriage, it had struck him that she'd never actually answered most of his questions. "I believe she's got those letters, and she knows exactly where Eunice Ogier is."

"So what should we do?"

Paix handed him the warrant application. "Well, first, we should start process for a warrant, to seize the letters before she has them destroyed —"

Commander Green set the warrant application on his desk. "Now wait just a minute —"

"And we should certainly tell Mrs. Spadros that this is going on in her household."

"That I agree with."

Paix blinked, surprised. "You want me to return there?"

"Of course! This is your case, is it not? I can't pull Kanhu to do this. The man is swarmed with homicides. It's too late to go now, but this shouldn't wait for Monday. Visit our Lady tomorrow afternoon, tell her what you've learned, then return here. I'll take care of the rest."

Paix felt relieved, and encouraged. He thought it would be much more difficult to get a warrant than that. "Yes, Commander. Thank you, Commander."

He bounded down the stairs towards his desk, excited at the prospect. In his twenty years on the force, he'd never been able to get a warrant served against the Spadros Family.

"You look like you've won the jackpot," C.K. said as Paix passed by.

"I feel it," Paix said. "By all the gods, I do feel it. I'll tell you all about it later." He rushed out to find a wagon so he might rejoin Briscola and Lightner. But their wagon was just pulling in.

Briscola seemed doubtful at the news. "You really think they'll serve warrant on our Family?"

"It's just a maid at the Country House," Paix said. "But it's a start. You'll see. Green doesn't like the way they get away with things any more than I do."

By the time Paix had updated his reports and reached home it was well past nightfall. Reina lay in bed, raising her head sleepily and smiled. "You're home."

Paix went over to kiss her forehead. "I am." He began putting his uniform away.

"Dinner's in the oven." Her head slumped into the pillow as her eyes closed.

She's had as long a day as mine. He pulled the covers over her, tucking them around her, then kissed her hair.

Paix ate his dinner, lay in bed beside Reina. But the feeling of unease he'd had at the elderly maid's home stayed with him.

Miss Call lied to me. She hid something. But what?

He was beginning to think Eunice Ogier was much more important to this case than he'd suspected.

* * *

The Commander had told Paix he had to work Saturdays helping C.K., so he went in the next day. Not being on shift, he showed up around nine and no one complained. C.K. looked up from his desk and laughed. "Green got you in here after all."

Paix grinned. "He did."

The boys' folders lay in a stack on his desk. It appeared C.K. had been assigned the most recent of the murdered boys as well.

Moving his typewriter to the floor, for the next several hours, Paix went through them. Photos, list of evidence, prints ....

A shoe print photo looked familiar.

Paix pulled out the shoe print photographs from each of the crime scenes. "Cartas."

C.K. looked up. "What?"

"The prints match. All the crime scenes. He's wearing the same shoes."

C.K. got up and hurried over, while Paix spread the photos out. "There's David Bryce. There's Caddy. There's Herbert."

"Good gods," C.K. said. He rushed back to his desk, pulled out a ruler. "Give me any with both feet showing."

Paix couldn't find any. He paged through the files, scribbling the case numbers on a pad, then went to the front desk. "Is Mr. Roberts in today? The photographer?"

The clerk gestured with his chin.

Paix went to the back of the station and down a hall to a door marked "Light Room" and knocked.

"Come in."

Photographs dripped on wires spread along the walls. The smell of damp chemicals hung in the air. Martin Roberts stood by a large table in the middle of the room with his shirt sleeves rolled up, a full apron covering his front. His dark skin shone with sweat. "Good day, Constable. How may I help?"

"I'm helping with the missing and murdered boys. Do you have any further shoe-prints? I'm looking for ones where you see both feet."

He chuckled, going to a file cabinet. "I may. You can only fit so many photos in those envelopes. You have the case numbers?"

Paix handed him the list, and the photographer began pulling out thick envelopes full of photos. Dividing the envelopes between them, the two paged through them.

"Here's one," Mr. Roberts said, handing it over. "You think these murders are related?"

"We do," Paix said. "Thanks ever so much."

The photographer grinned. "My pleasure. I'll put these away; just put that one in the file when you're done."

Paix hurried back to the main hall with the photo. C.K. took it to his desk, scribbling calculations on a pad as Paix watched. Then C.K. nodded. "I knew he gave Herbert Bryce his clothes!" He looked up. "This confirms his height, Hanger." He pulled out an old portrait of Crab, marked with his height. "The same."

Something about this wasn't right. Could this man be crafty enough to choose Crab simply because they were the same height? "I don't think Crab could fit in the clothes Herbert wore."

"He gave him old ones, Hanger, I'm sure of it. Too bad we didn't measure Crab's hands or shoe size ...." C.K.'s voice trailed away. Then he glanced up at the clock. "Aren't you supposed to go visit our Lady?"

Paix had completely forgotten. "Get something to eat," he said, "and I'll visit Mrs. Spadros. I shouldn't be gone long — we can work on this more later."

* * *

"Our Lady is still at luncheon," the butler said, "which is fortunate, as we must speak."

"Very well," Paix said.

"You are forbidden to sit in the presence of the Lady, no matter what she tells you. We discussed this last time, yet you defied my warning."

"She invited me to sit. I didn't wish to cause offense."

The man's tone turned lecturing. "Mrs. Spadros is of an amiable nature. Do not seek to take advantage."

Paix felt shocked. "I would never do such a thing!"

The butler didn't seem impressed. "Remember your place, Constable. This is our Lady of Spadros. You are far from her equal, and must never forget it, either by word or deed."

Dismayed, Paix said, "I understand."

"You may wait in the parlor now."

Paix stood in front of the fireplace at parade rest for a few moments, relishing the warmth.

Mrs. Jacqueline Spadros entered, today wearing no veil. She had a lovely face, and Paix wondered why she hid it before. "Yes, Constable, how may I help you?" She gestured for him to sit. "Would you like some tea?"

"No, mum." He certainly would **not** sit, not after the dressing-down that butler had given him. "Were you aware, mum, that letters were being sent from Eunice Ogier to the Spadros Country House?"

Mrs. Spadros frowned. "Eunice ... Ogier .... Is that the woman you came here about last time?"

"Yes, mum. Apparently she was known by a member of your kitchen staff at the Country House."

"I shall speak to the staff about this at once."

For a brief instant, Paix felt at a loss for words. "Yes, well, the woman said Miss Ogier left the city. I thought you should know."

"Thank you for telling me. Is anything else required?"

A young, rich woman ... the day Mrs. Spadros was with a large group ... and the messenger boy said the letter came from Spadros Manor ....

My dear little Jacqui, is it you?

Could Mrs. Spadros herself have spoken to the boy, using an alias? "Do you have mourning garb?"

She seemed uncomfortable, spoke too brightly. "Why, no, I have never needed to purchase any. I have been most fortunate in that regard."

Paix nodded, sure there was more to this than she was saying. "Yes. That is most fortunate." He now regretted coming here. She was in the Family — no matter what she knew, she'd never tell him anything. "Well, I'm sure you're quite busy. Good day, mum."

When Paix returned to the station, C.K. approached him, face glum. "I have terrible news. They found Stephen Rivers. Dead."

17

Paix felt horrified. "How?"

C.K. shook his head mournfully. "Strangled, like the rest. The same man, from the looks of it. Why'd I let the boy return home?"

"It's not your fault, Cartas! This scoundrel must have found the boy after he left home." Why would Stephen leave his home, when an officer stood guard? "Come on, I'll buy you a drink."

The Straight Flush was a police bar, empty this time of day, but a nightly haunt for the Probationaries quartered at the barracks next door to the station. The owner — who was also the bartender during the day — smiled when he saw them. "What can I get you?"

"I'll have beer," Paix said, "and get him whatever he wants."

"Double vodka," C.K. said. "Been a bad day."

"That'll cheer you," the man said.

Paix and C.K. found a table, and the owner brought them their drinks.

"Cartas, the boy ran off after we warned him not to. You even gave him a dime!"

C.K. didn't touch his drink, only shook his head. "It's something about this case. All these cases. I feel like Crab is blocks ahead of me." A look came to C.K.'s eyes that Paix had never seen in them before: desperation. He drained his glass. "I'm drowning in bodies. And I don't think I can do anything to stop it."

"Sure you can," Paix said. "The Commander is getting a warrant to search for the letters Eunice Ogier sent to the Spadros Country House."

C.K. sat gaping at him.

"The woman Stephen Rivers said asked for David Bryce."

C.K. nodded.

"Don't you see? With even one of those letters, we can find this woman. Talk with her, find out what she knows." Paix felt sure Eunice Ogier — whoever she really was — hadn't left the city as Miss Call said. "We'll stop this man, you'll see."

"He's really getting a warrant? Against the Spadros Family?"

"He told me he'd take care of everything."

"I'm astonished," C.K. said, a glimmer of hope in his eyes. "It won't do much, but if we can get their help, it'll be a good start."

But when they returned to the station, the Commander was there. He gave them the bad news: there would be no warrant. Not now, not ever.

C.K. slunk off, dejected. Paix was furious. "How long are we going to toady to these men? Someone is killing their boys and they'll do nothing?"

"Just wait," the Commander said. "There are still things I can do. We must tread carefully here."

"Look," Paix said. "I understand your position. Your bosses answer to the Family. But a villain's loose. He's taken eight boys now, and three are dead. We set our only suspect free, and the only real informant we have might be destroying our only way to contact a woman who may be our only living witness. We have to find those letters!"

Commander Green said, "You have this hope to just storm in there and get things sorted, but it doesn't work that way. Don't you think it'd be much better to ask for their help, to work with them, rather than agitate them?"

"No! Are we the law, or not?"

Green shook his head. "You don't understand —"

"I understand perfectly. You believe working with these criminals is more important than saving a child's life. I believe that's wrong. I didn't sign up for this."

"That's where you're wrong, Hanger. You signed up for this job on your own free will. So you have two choices: resign, or follow my orders." He let out a breath. "I looked up your file today. Do you ever want your shield back? Then you're going to have to let go of this irrational hatred of the Families!" He paused, as if searching for a different line of play. "I can help you, if you're wiling to play along. I know you're no maniac, Hanger — you're capable of making the right play. I can't force you to trust me. But I'm asking you to. Can you do that?"

At first, Paix wasn't sure. But he took a breath, let it out. Then he nodded.

"Now finish your work, and let me see what I can do."

Paix didn't trust himself to speak, so he saluted and left.

C.K. sat slumped in his chair in front of the stacks of cases. "I don't know what the use of any of this is anymore. Why do we even ask for warrants when we can never get any? Why not let them all kill each other and be done with it?"

Paix drew up a chair from the neighboring desk and sat beside him, remembering what the Commander had said long ago. "Because we're cops, that's why. The people out there need us to do our best for them." He clapped C.K. on the shoulder. "Find an easy one and work on that for a while. Forget about these boys for a while."

C.K. turned anguished eyes to him. "But how can I? How many more are going to die while we play police here?"

Paix gave him a one-shoulder shrug. "The Commander seemed to have some ideas he was working on."

C.K. nodded, his shoulders straightening. Then he took a deep breath, let it out. "I can do this."

"You can." Paix rose, returned the chair. "One thing at a time, right? Find an easy one."

C.K. snorted.

"Or at least something easy to move things forward." Paix picked up the nearest file, opened it. "Here, you still need the coroner's report on this one." He closed it, set it on the desk. "Walk over there and ask the clerk to check on it." Paix surveyed the overflowing desk. "Make a pile of ones which need things done, and others where you're waiting for someone else. I'll take the files for these boys."

"Thanks, Hanger." C.K.'s shoulders slumped. "You think they'll ever give me another partner?"

Paix grinned. "If I wasn't already in the discard pile I'd apply for the job. But someone should come along soon enough."

He walked away leaving C.K. sorting through his files. But Paix didn't feel the hope he tried to give to his friend.

You have two choices: resign, or follow my orders.

Paix went home.

* * *

Reina was just starting dinner: a stew. She smiled when he came in. "You're home early!"

He kissed her, feeling uneasy. *You're capable of making the right play.* But what was the right play here?

She scooped all the bits of meat and vegetable into the pot, filled it with water, and set it to cook. "Are you well?"

Paix blinked. "I think so. Why?"

She began wiping down the counter. "You're just standing there. And you're still wearing your uniform."

Paix chuckled. "I suppose I am." He took off his uniform, then changed into street clothes. "Let's go for a walk."

Reina glanced up in surprise. "Let me change." She turned the heat down on the stove.

Paix sat watching her undress, the curves of her body.

No one ever questions a dream when they're in it.

Reina turned to him, dressed and ready. "Let's go."

They strolled along for a while in the twilight. Paix said, "May I ask something?"

"Of course."

"What happened with you and Jake? Really?"

Reina sighed. "After he got fired, we had to sell everything just to eat. Jake refused to go to the Families, and no one else wanted a man dismissed for violence."

Paix said nothing, hoping she would explain why she hadn't stood by him.

Finally, she continued: "Then Jake started his private detective business. But some of his clients frightened me." She stopped walking, her face pale in the streetlight. "He's in with scoundrels, Paix, the worst kind."

Paix felt stunned. "Did you speak to him about this?"

"I tried, many a time." She went silent for a few steps, then said, "One in particular ... his name's Frank ... the man gives me a feeling of dread. But Jake believes in him, more than I've ever seen him believe in anyone. I told Jake he must choose: me or him." She turned away. "But he won't listen. He has an answer for everything. The man pays well. He's trustworthy, honorable. They have such fun together." She snorted. "I make it sound a romance affair, but no, it's not that. I would know if it were that. It's like this man has him completely deceived." She shook her head. "I had to get out. I — I won't watch Jake die." At that, her voice broke. "I love him too much, even still, to watch him die. And yet I know that's where this game ends."

Paix stood still, mind utterly blank. "Why are you with me?"

"Oh, Paix," she said, "it's not like that."

"Isn't it? How is this different from the Cathedral?"

Reina gaped at him. "How can you say such a thing?"

"Do you love me?"

"Yes!"

"Or is this some life or death choice?"

"I love you," Reina whispered, her tears glinting. "I love you."

Paix turned away. "You can stay as long as you like. But I'll not have you pay with your body, your service, or anything else."

Paix considered sleeping on the floor, but decided against it. This was his home, and he'd sleep where he wished.

He lay turned away from her, listening first to her sobs then her soft breathing.

But he couldn't sleep through his grief, his dread, his remorse.

What was the truth here? What had he done? What had Jake gotten involved with?

18

When Paix woke, Reina had made breakfast. But he couldn't look at her, and food had lost its appeal. He dressed in street clothes. "I'm going out."

"Paix, please, don't do this."

He put his hand on the doorpost, leaned his forehead upon his arm. "Jake Bower has saved my life more than once. He trusted me, and I repaid him with betrayal. I'll not let him die without trying to stop it."

Jake had moved, and it took going to Jake's parents' home in the Legal District to get his address. Paix found Jake close by, in a small one-bedroom apartment which doubled as his office.

The instant he saw Paix, Jake punched him in the face. "That's for getting me arrested."

Surprised, Paix wobbled several steps backwards from the blow. He picked up his cap from the ground and straightened, rubbing the side of his face. "I never told them to do that. When I woke, I told them you **couldn't** have done it."

This seemed to calm Jake, and he stepped back to let Paix in.

Jake and Reina's dark wood oval dining table nearly filled the front room; bookshelves and file cases lined the walls. A small desk stood underneath the front window. A door to the left was shut; a short hallway lay straight ahead. "You've gone back to scribing," Paix said.

Jake nodded, a slight smile on his face. "My father's trade. It's the only thing I was ever really good at." He gestured at the table. "Sit down."

Paix dropped his cap on the table and sat.

Jake sat across from him, folded his hands on the table. "I took your advice. The house held too many memories." He sat silent for a moment, then said, "What do you want?"

"You wanted to know why Reina left."

Jake leaned forward. "And?"

Paix considered the matter. "She's afraid of one of your clients. She fears the man will end you. She said, 'I love Jake too much to watch him die.' For gods' sake — what's going on?"

Jake's eyes narrowed. "Which man?"

Paix scoffed. "You know which man! Frank. She said she told you to choose, and when you chose him she felt she had to leave."

"That's ridiculous," Jake said, yet Paix knew Jake lied.

Paix rose, disgusted. "I had to see this for myself. Who is this man, and why is his favor more important than your wife's?"

Jake stood, became earnest. "Things are changing in Bridges. Frank and his men helped me move, got me good clients. He's even given me leads about my daughter's death. I just have one last job to do for him, and I'll be done with that in a couple of days. You tell her that." He glanced away. "But even if he hadn't helped me, I'd support him. I do support him." Jake grabbed Paix by the upper arms. "He has a real plan to get rid of the Families. We can get our city back!"

For an instant, Paix felt interested, excited even. But something warned him against it. The fevered light in Jake's eyes when he spoke of this man Frank was only part of it. The deception, the way he'd pushed his wife away .... "Who is he? Where does he live? Why is he helping you? For that matter, where does he get money to help you?"

Jake glanced aside. "None of that's important. People call him Frank, but that's just what they call him. He goes by other names too. He's a wealthy man, with real power. But he's got to be careful." Jake looked around, as if someone might be listening outside his door at half past ten on a Sunday. "There are those wishing him dead."

"For going against the Families?"

Jake nodded earnestly. "And more. People have tried to kill him many a time."

That last rang true. Paix remembered the joke he'd made with Briscola. *They might miss.* Is that why Reina thought Jake's association with this man might kill him? "This doesn't feel right."

Jake bristled, his hands dropping to his sides. "I know what I'm doing."

"Just be careful. Please?"

"I'm always careful. And you tell my wife to come home. She has nothing to be afraid of. If she doesn't want Frank to come over, I'll meet him somewhere else."

I love him too much to watch him die.

In a flash, Paix understood. "What's this job you're doing?"

Jake told him.

"Don't do it," Paix said. "Reina's right. If you do this and someone finds out, you're dead."

Jake laughed. "I've done it more than once. It's fun!" His smile faded as he peered at Paix. "Thank you for coming here, for telling me this." He scoffed, shook his head. "It's so very clear now. You two deserve each other, with your constant worry and your preoccupation with how things 'feel.' It's pathological."

Paix stood there, unable to make sense of what Jake was saying. "So you'll let Reina go?"

"You're actually serious." Jake snorted in disbelief. "No. Of course not! I took a vow. Perhaps you don't understand that. She's my wife, for better or worse, until death parts us." He let out a breath, his shoulders slumping. "I thought you were my friend. And even though I knew your motives were completely self-serving, I took your advice: I let it go. I won't bother either of you again. But I'm sure as hell not going to put her through a divorce. I'm neither petty nor cruel enough to subject her to public humiliation and scorn for her whoredom. If you love her, why would you want me to?" He leaned forward. "And because I care about you, even after everything you've done, I won't destroy your reputation and career over it either."

Then he straightened. "You know what? I pity you, Hanger. I truly do. One day, she'll tire of you, and you'll be left with nothing, the same as the day you met her. If she truly loved you, she'd release you to court a woman who can give you the son you so long for."

Paix stared at Jake, speechless. It was like some other person had taken the form of the man he'd known for the last eighteen years. "What **happened** to you?"

Jake put his hand to his chin for a moment, then their eyes met. "Why, I suppose **you** did."

Paix found himself stumbling along a side street, not caring where he went. He gazed up at his apartment building, and sat himself at a bench across the way. He felt overwhelmed.

"Constable?" Martin Roberts, the photographer from the precinct, stood there with a woman a bit darker-skinned than himself, who pushed a pram. "Don't mean to disturb you; I just wanted to say hello." He held out his hand.

Paix rose, and they shook hands. "What brings you out here?"

"Paperwork," Roberts said. "I'm being transferred to Precinct 7." He gave a broad smile. "Much closer to home. We decided since I had to come all the way out here, we'd celebrate with an outing." He gestured to the woman beside him. "Mrs. Roberts, and our new son."

Paix tipped his cap at the woman. "A pleasure." He turned to Mr. Roberts. "And congratulations. I guessed you'd be leaving us soon. You do fine work."

"Thank you, Constable. Just wanted to say hello. We'll be on our way."

Paix sat on the bench. *Everything's changing.* He was no closer to knowing what to do — about David's disappearance, those boys' murders, or even Reina — than when he left.

Paix went up to his room, knocked, let himself in.

Reina rushed to him. "I was worried for you. Are you well?"

Paix shrugged. "I went to see Jake. It's like he's someone I never knew." He went to a chair, sat heavily. "Did **I** do this?"

Reina knelt before him, took hold of his arms. "No. Don't blame yourself. He's been like this long before I left." Her gaze turned aside. "It was our girl's death that did it. At least, that's when it started. And now he's in with these men. He's completely lost his way."

Moved, Paix touched the side of her face, took her chin. "What are we going to do?"

"I'll do whatever you need me to."

That's the problem. He shook his head, put his face in his hands. "This isn't going to work, Reina. I can't live like this, wondering if you're here because you love me or if you just want a place to stay."

"I do love you. I've loved you for the past two years. I have a place to stay — more than one now, if you count Heap and Lane's place. If I just wanted to be safe, I could have joined the Dealers." She paused, head down for a moment, then gazed in his eyes. "But I came to you. I promise you, I'm here because I want to be. Because I love you." She cradled his face in her hands. "I won't go back to him. I can't. But if you want me to leave, I will."

Suddenly, Paix needed to get away from this room, this woman. He rose, began to change into his uniform. "I have work to do."

* * *

Paix went to the beat station first, just to check in, then found the neighbor who'd said Herbert Bryce had asked for money.

"That was some time ago, Constable," the man said.

"Do you recall who he said he needed to pay?"

"Some rich woman, if I recall. She wouldn't help until they paid her."

A rich woman. "Did he say how she might help?"

"No, Constable, he didn't."

Paix then went to the precinct station. It had been many years since he'd worked on a Sunday. The precinct station was quieter, emptier than usual.

C.K.'s desk stood empty.

Paix had a vision of C.K. sitting in his ratty chair at his unkempt home with his disheveled wife, drinking.

The missing boys' files were where Paix put them the day before. The murdered boys' files were on C.K.'s desk. Paix went through the files one by one.

There was no mention of a rich woman asking the other families for money in exchange for her help. But then, no one would think to ask.

Eunice Ogier was part of this. He could feel it. And a scenario formed in his mind.

A twelve year old boy. A nice, rich lady — twenty, or perhaps thirty — wants to talk to him, have him do something for her, maybe even offers him money. He's flattered, dazzled by the attention, perhaps hopeful that this will solve his mother's financial problems. He walks off a bit with this woman. Then at least one man grabs him, covering his mouth so he can't scream.

She goes to the family, offers to help them — **if** they pay her.

A sweet little set-up, particularly if the man liked strangling.

The real flaw in this scenario was Caddy Arrenegada. The other boys were fatherless, their widowed mothers ripe for such a scam. But Caddy's father was an Associate. He'd never hire a woman. He'd either take matters into his own hands, or go to the Family for help.

But Caddy was the first to die.

I didn't do this, Hanger, I swear.

Paix frowned. Why did Caddy and his friends beat them with bricks? Why blame Sheinwold for it?

Who benefitted from Sheinwold being kicked off the force?

It was a trap.

Could this possibly be connected with the woman who tried to kill Sheinwold? Could **she** have planned the attack?

Sheinwold said the first partner disappeared. What if this red-haired outsider woman wasn't a Fed at all?

Could **she** be Eunice Ogier? Whoever she was, she now had a truck full of Tommy-guns. And perhaps this man who liked to strangle was her new partner.

This whole thing with her began at least two years ago. What were they planning?

Fear gnawed at his gut. This could just be a multiple murderer and his woman — that was bad enough. Or this could be far bigger than any of them imagined.

The death of a Detective Constable who worked for the Family would be noted, investigated, avenged. But a Wharf Patrol man who sent boys to attack cops and collaborated with the Feds wouldn't be mourned by anyone.

If this woman hired Caddy and his boys to attack them with bricks, the boys knew her face. Probably her partner's face as well.

None of those boys would survive.

Eunice Ogier had to be rich. She had money for the zeppelin, assuming the old woman's story was true. She was connected with the Spadros Family: the letter the messenger boy brought to the Spadros Country House came from Spadros Manor.

He considered the evasions he'd faced from Mrs. Jacqueline Spadros the two times he visited the Manor. She knew this Eunice Ogier. She knew exactly where the woman was. The Family had no regard for the police; Jacqueline Spadros likely felt a duty to cover for her.

If the letters weren't already destroyed, they soon would be.

Could the Lady of Spadros possibly be involved with these disappearances and murders?

There was no way to know for certain. But they had more than reasonable suspicion to get a warrant to search Miss Call's cottage.

We could find Eunice Ogier — if we were allowed to do our jobs, instead of pandering to the Families.

Leaving the eight files on his desk, Paix took the wagon to Market Center, then walked to the Grand Fountain in the center of the island.

He sat on a bench. People passed by: determined, important, surrounded by City Hall, the Ballroom, the Courthouse, the Opera House, all the buildings of a city as ruined inside as the Pot.

How many more are going to die while we play police here?

Suddenly, Paix had his answer. No more.

No more pandering to the Families.

No more playing by the rules.

He would get those letters, no matter what.

19

Eventually, Paix returned home. The rest of the day, he considered the matter.

He still had the slip the Commander gave him. If he covered the date with his thumb, the driver might not question it. That gave him a way to the Country House.

The woman was blind. And what did she say? *Eight, twelve, four, and eight.*

If he were to arrive at, say, half past two, that would give time to search with no one the wiser.

He couldn't involve C.K., Briscola, or Lightner in this — it would ruin their careers. To go alone was the height of folly. But who could he involve in this?

Once Reina lay sleeping, Paix went to find Sheinwold.

* * *

Even at this hour on a Sunday, there were lines at the bridge to Spadros.

"Carriage search," the guard said. "What are you doing out?"

"Night duty at the mill," Paix said, keeping his voice low enough the driver wouldn't hear. "I'm well late as it is."

"I'll say," the guard said. "Have a pleasant evening."

The taxi deposited him at the wharf near west 1st Street. Lights blazed on the Promenade. as revelers staggered along. The shops were closing, and lamps swung far out on the pier.

Paix hurried over. "I'm looking for Albert Sheinwold."

"You and an army," one of the men said. "He's late." The man peered past. "Oh, there he is."

A large figure stood backlit by the streetlights, wearing a cap and carrying an unlit lamp. "Who wants me?"

Paix moved into the light. "It's just me, Al. Can we talk?"

Sheinwold nodded, moving out towards a bench on the pier.

A man called back, "Don't take forever, Sheinwold, we got a job to do."

When Sheinwold got to the bench, Paix said, "Where have you been?"

Sheinwold shrugged. "I figured the chance of you being followed was pretty good. Besides, I like to keep moving. Surprised you found me."

"You want to put a stick in the wheel of the lot of them?"

"Depends on who you mean."

Paix told him his plan.

Sheinwold looked astonished. "Are you crazy? Not only are you harassing a Spadros retainer, you're forging a warrant!"

"Well, not really — the woman is blind, so —"

"You're going to lie to a blind woman? Frighten her into letting you search her home? You can't be serious." He paused for a moment. "What's happened to you, Hanger?"

"What's happened is that I'm tired of the Spadros Family doing whatever it likes and getting away with it. You know who's our number one suspect in these strangle murders? That new Associate Crab."

"Aw, Crab couldn't strangle a fly, Hanger!"

"And we had him dead to rights, but then that Sawbuck got him out before we could get our witness to the lineup. And now two more boys are dead."

Sheinwold gaped at him. "You need to slow down, Hanger. I mean it. Just — will you take a day and think about it?"

"I've been thinking about it since yesterday. But I need your help. Are you in?"

"Hell, no," Sheinwold said. "If this was only to get back at the force for what they did to me, I'd be on it in a heartbeat. But you couldn't pay me to go against the Family. I like living too much."

"So you won't help me."

Sheinwold hesitated. "Can I think about it?"

"Sure. But don't take too long."

"I'll meet you outside the station before briefing tomorrow."

* * *

Paix went back to bed, but didn't sleep well. Was he doing the right thing?

I won't frighten the old lady. I'll go in polite as can be.

He rose early, got to the station well before briefing.

"Psst," Sheinwold said from behind. He peered out from around the corner of the building, gesturing Paix over. "Don't want to be seen here."

"So what did you decide?"

"Sorry, Hanger," he said. "I'm not doing it. I'll ride there with you if you want and keep an eye out, but I'll not go in."

"Well," Paix said, "that'll be enough. I want to leave here at luncheon, so we can get there by half past 2."

Sheinwold nodded. "I'll be over by the Badugi Bistro right here off Snow." He pointed down the street. "Have the driver stop there, like you're getting something, and I'll hop in."

"Sounds good." He almost turned away, but then said, "Thanks, Al. I appreciate it."

Sheinwold gave a wry smile. "I always did live dangerous."

Paix went about his day with his men, telling them around mid-day that he needed to meet up with C.K. at the station. From there, he ate a quick and early luncheon then went into the station.

C.K. peered at him. "Whatcha doing here?"

"Need a new citation book, just used up the last page."

C.K. let out a short laugh, then went back to reading his file. Paix grabbed a copy of a report from one of the files on his desk, then folded it neatly, put it in the breast pocket of his jacket, and went outside.

A wagon sat there, the driver eating his luncheon.

"Got a request to the Spadros Country House," Paix told the driver, waving Commander Green's old slip. "Right away."

The man sighed, dejected. "I don't even get to eat?" He began packing up his lunch pail.

"The Commander called it urgent. If it makes you feel any better, I didn't eat either," Paix said. "Would you mind if I went by Badugi first?"

"Naw," the driver said, as he climbed aboard. "Can't have a

Constable faint in the line of duty."

Paix chuckled and stepped inside the carriage. Around the corner, the carriage stopped, and Shenwold came to the door. Paix got out at the same time as Sheinwold got in.

Paix bought a drink and a roll from the stand outside, then glanced behind him. The driver was busy eating and hadn't noticed a thing.

Paix climbed back in the carriage. Sheinwold lay sprawled across the bench seat, opening an eye when Paix entered.

Paix put his finger to his lips, then took the speaker tube. "Ride on, if you will."

"Spadros Country House, yes, Constable."

Paix spoke in Sheinwold's ear. "You hungry?"

He yawned. "Ate already, thanks."

So Paix munched the roll while they rode along.

He checked his pocketwatch. They had to be gone when the nursemaid arrived at four, or it would all be for nothing. He took up the speaker tube. "Can you go faster? I must be back to report to the Commander before he leaves for home."

"Yes, sir," the driver said, and a "yaaah!" came from in front, the carriage moving faster.

"You're unbelievable," Sheinwold said. "You never used to lie like this." He closed his eyes, shaking his head.

Paix didn't care. He'd waited too long as it was.

When they got there, Paix nudged Sheinwold. "Get out, or hide? If he comes back here, he'll see you."

"I'll watch at the door like I said."

"Be ready to get out, then." He took up the tube. "Don't go to the door — stop at the stand of trees about a hundred yards east of the main entry."

"Yes, Constable."

Sheinwold sat up muttering, yet he sprang out along with Paix. The driver yelled, "Hey, what's going on there?"

The carriage must've wobbled strangely, Paix thought. It was the only way he could have known something wasn't right. "Sorry," Paix said. "Stumbled a bit."

"Careful there, Constable," the driver said, his voice amused.

"I'll wait here."

Paix turned to Sheinwold. "Keep out of his sight."

Sheinwold nodded, angling away and around to follow.

Paix went directly to the old woman's home and knocked. "Who is it?"

"Constable Hanger of the Central Bridges Police Department." Paix glanced over; Sheinwold crossed to the side of the house with a "what the hell are you doing" look on his face. "We have a warrant to search the premises."

Tapping of wood on wood, then the door opened. The old woman stood staring blankly. "But why? What have I done?"

He pulled out the paper, waved it so it crinkled. "I'm sorry, Miss Call, but you must let us in. We have a court order."

She began to call out. "Mr. Simpson? Are you there? Who are these men?"

That must be the butler's name, Paix thought. "It's all right, Miss Call, just step aside and we'll be —"

"No! Help! Help!"

"This is ridiculous." Sheinwold pushed past, knocking her aside. "Get what you came for and let's go."

The old woman leaned up against the wall wailing, sobbing.

An instant of remorse struck. "I'm sorry," Paix said. "Where are your letters?"

She pointed to a writing-desk, and Paix went to it, rifling through them. None of them had the name Eunice Ogier on them. He turned to Sheinwold. "Search the place. I'm looking for letters to a Eunice Ogier."

Sheinwold pulled cushions off the sofa, rummaged through drawers while the woman sobbed. He shook his head. "Nothing."

Footsteps from far off. "We better go," Paix said. He put a hand on the woman's shoulder but she shook it off. "I'm so sorry."

"Curse you, coppers! Burn in the Fire!" She spat in his direction. "My people will skin you live, and all your kin!"

Terror struck for Reina, his family. What had he done?

Sheinwold pulled at his sleeve. "Run, you fool, before their men get here!"

They ran for the carriage. "Full speed to the station," Paix yelled, then they jumped inside the carriage. Men came out of the entryway, shouting as they receded in the distance.

"Now you've done it," Sheinwold muttered. "I hope you like pulling bodies from the water. That is, if they don't kill you first. Whatever possessed you to give your real name?"

Dismayed, Paix put his head in his hands. "I don't know. She asked, and I — I didn't want to lie."

"For gods' sake, Hanger! You just falsified a warrant against Spadros Family property. You tricked and frightened an old blind woman, disheveled her home. And you balk at lying?" He let out a short laugh, shaking his head. "You can't be half in this anymore." He leaned back, hands behind his head. "As soon as they get your name out of her, they'll be after you. I can get a message to Reina. You want to stay at my place tonight?"

Paix peered at him. "Sure. But don't frighten her, okay?" He pointed at the scar on his forehead. "I forgot to tell her you didn't do this."

Sheinwold scoffed. "Right."

* * *

Paix hid outside the station behind bushes in the twilight. How could he account for his day? What could he possibly write about what happened?

You've been a fool, he told himself. But he now felt in a dilemma. Writing the truth was impossible. Lying on a report was equally impossible.

"What are you doing?" Briscola stood squinting at him.

Paix felt foolish. "Nature calls."

"For gods' sake," Briscola said. "Outside the station?" He scoffed, turning away. "We're having a party across the way for Lightner. It's his last day. Want to come?"

"Let me do my reports then I'll be over."

"I'm gonna miss that kid," Briscola said.

He chuckled as Briscola walked off: Briscola wasn't all that much older than Lightner.

Paix didn't trust Sheinwold to get a message to Reina without scaring her half to death, so he went to the messenger booth. "I need a Memory Boy. I'll be inside."

"Right away, Constable."

Everyone bustled about the precinct station as usual. No one looked at him oddly or cried out his name.

He sat at his desk. *The driver knew we went there. He'll make his own report.*

Paix wrote his morning beat reports from his notes, then concocted a tale of going to the woman's home, knocking, finding no one there, then being chased off by Spadros men.

It might work. But he didn't place too much hope in it. Where would Reina be safe?

"Hello, Constable Hanger."

The little blond boy and his guards stood before the desk. Paix felt surprised. "That was fast."

"I was on my way here," the Memory Boy said. "I have a message from the Cathedral."

"Oh," Paix said. He glanced around; no one stood by. The two boys had withdrawn, backs turned, to survey the room. "What did they say?"

"The Cathedral sends its regards and thanks you for your honor. You and your man have credit here."

Paix blinked, confused. "Is that all?" After over a month's silence, he expected more.

"Yes, Constable. How can I help you?"

Paix glanced at the two older boys, who still faced the room. "I need two messages sent." One he sent to his parents, warning them he'd gotten in trouble with the Family. The other he sent to Reina. "Sheinwold's innocent. I'm in Family trouble. Go somewhere safe. I love you."

The boy nodded. "Which one first?"

"The second. And hurry." He gave the boy an extra penny.

The little boy smiled. "I thought so." He turned to his guards. "We're going for a ride!"

After the boys left, Paix stood outside the station in the darkness past the lamplights. Should he go to the party?

I never go to parties. The Family might not expect me to be there.

He crossed the street, peered in. The obnoxious Probationary was inside, laughing with the crowd.

He didn't feel much like a party, not tonight.

Briscola came outside. "What are you doing out here?"

Paix shook his head, staring at nothing. "I'm in trouble, Leone. Bad trouble."

"You mean like with the Family?"

Paix nodded. "Give Lightner my regards, but privately. If anyone else asks, you didn't see me since before luncheon." He looked at the younger man, feeling a surge of sadness. "You're a good man. Do whatever you have to do to get out of this precinct." He faced the street. "Don't end up like me."

He felt Briscola's hand on his shoulder. "Constable, I — I don't know what's going on. But you have friends here. Let us help."

Paix smiled, feeling bitter. He had no friends here, not anymore. "Thanks." He walked down the street, feeling Briscola's gaze upon him.

Paix walked the wharf side of the Promenade, neither knowing nor caring where he went. He found himself sitting on a bench by the huge statue of Acevedo Spadros I, staring out over the water as the sky lightened. The only thing which kept him from casting himself into it, swimming to the Suction to die in the undertow, was Reina.

Even though he knew he was a fool for loving Reina, he still did. More than anything.

"I thought I'd find you here," Sheinwold said. He had a black eye and a bandage on his right hand. He plopped himself down on the bench. "Bad news is they know it was you. Good news is they only kicked it up to the Heir. Roy Spadros isn't after you — at least, not yet."

Paix shrugged. They were all the same, those lot. "Sorry you got hell for it."

Sheinwold let out a short laugh, wincing. "This? That's nothing. That's just for not stopping you, not that I knew what you were gonna do." He gave a sly wink and a grin. "I knew they wouldn't rough me up too much — after you came to me the other night, I decided fuck the police, and the Wharf Patrol too."

"So what did you do?"

"Joined the Family full-time, you nit." He grinned. "I always liked being an enforcer better than cleaning up after it anyway."

For some reason, this didn't bother Paix as much as he thought it would have.

"Oh, and Reina says hello. I told you I wouldn't scare her."

So the Memory Boy got to her first. Paix felt relieved. "Thanks." He stared glumly out over the water. "I'm done for, aren't I?"

"Pretty much. But you knew that when you went on that fool's mission."

"The old lady's destroyed the letters, I can feel it. And I don't think she told the truth about the woman leaving town, either."

Sheinwold said nothing.

How could he go back to the station after all this? Paix felt exhausted. "Eunice Ogier knows something about the boy gone missing. She might even be the one who took him. If I can just find her, I might find the boy." He put his head in his hands. "All these deaths ... they're related. I just know it. C.K. said they were the same man."

"Huh?"

Paix chuckled in spite of himself. "I forgot you didn't know." Then the weight of it all fell upon him. "This boy missing has turned into five boys missing and three strangled. C.K.'s convinced it's all the same man."

"Good gods!" Sheinwold looked horrified. "And this Ogier woman is involved in it."

Paix nodded. "She was our only real lead, other than Crab. C.K. thinks he did it."

"I shouldn't be telling you this, Hanger, but the Crab's in hot water. They're 'questioning' him in Spadros Manor." Sheinwold rubbed his nose. "But I don't think he did it."

Paix wasn't convinced Crab did it either.

Sheinwold said, "So whatcha gonna do?"

What could he do? Paix hadn't close to enough money to leave the city. So he had few options. He could try to evade the Family as long as he could — but this seemed cowardly. Besides, it left Reina and his family exposed, as either targets for retribution or to be taken as bait.

Or he could go back to work and let the cards play out.
He stood. "I guess I'll go back to work."

20

When he went into the station, Paix felt hunted, watched. But no one said a thing. In the pre-shift briefing, though, the Commander told them that the second of Caddy's friends had been found strangled.

"Kanhu, you're on this, obviously. And I've got a Detective Constable coming from Precinct 2 to help out."

Everyone glanced at each other, and Paix thought: *what did the poor guy do to deserve this?*

C.K. just nodded. By the way he moved, Paix suspected he'd been drinking already.

After the briefing, Paix went to C.K.. "You need help?"

"Naw, I sent a couple Probies to pick up Crab. We measure his hands, his feet, and it's a done deal."

"What about his team?"

"Look, Hanger, we get him, we stop the killing." C.K. swayed a bit. "I just want this to be over."

"I don't think it's him. And I think this is way bigger than we imagined. Let me send Briscola to patrol, and we can —"

"Will you just shut the fuck up? Leave me alone. I'm gonna book this guy when they get back, and then I'm gonna go across the street and celebrate."

So Paix and Briscola got into the wagon to the beat station, signed in, went walking across the street to begin their beat. But Paix felt watched, as if everyone knew what he'd done, knew he'd been marked for death.

"Constable?"

Briscola's question snapped Paix from his reverie. "Yes?"

"I — I just didn't expect to see you here today. After what you said last night. Should I be worried?"

"Hmm?"

"I mean, no offense, but — they might miss."

Paix began to laugh in spite of how he felt. "I'm sorry — you're right. We should split up. But somehow I doubt they'll try for me in broad daylight."

"I'd rather they didn't try for you at all."

"That can't be helped."

"But what did you do?"

Paix shook his head. "It's better you don't know. I'm sure you'll find out soon enough." He gestured with his chin. "Go on. Take 6th. I'll do the Hedge."

"Good luck, Constable." Briscola went off, shoulders hunched.

Paix walked down Snow Street to the Hedge, knowing his days were marked. But by some miracle, his day went well.

When Paix got back to the precinct station, C.K. was sitting on the steps, drunk out of his mind. "They can't find him," C.K. sobbed. "Crab's gone. More boys are gonna die."

Paix shrugged, patted C.K.'s shoulder. He couldn't tell the poor guy where Crab was — it'd put Sheinwold in hot water along with him. "They'll find him sooner or later."

"I just want this to be over. By all the gods, just let it be over."

Paix stopped a passing PC. "Take Detective Senior Constable Kanhu home, please."

The young man nodded. "Right away, Constable."

Paix went back to Market Center, in search of Reina.

He found her at Heap and Lane's house, and the three of them rushed to him when he arrived.

Reina burst into tears. "Oh, gods, I'm so glad you're alive!"

"As am I," Paix said.

"Come sit and have dinner," Lane said. "I paid your maid for a week and gave her a holiday."

For an instant Paix felt confused.

"Oh," he finally said. "Thank you."

Lane gave him an amused smile. "I set up a bed in the room the boys used to have, and Reina's already in the girls' room."

"Thank you," Paix said, "but I don't think I should stay here. It might only bring you trouble."

Heap said, "But where will you go?"

"Home," Paix said. "If they can find me plainly, they won't bother any of you over it."

"Oh, Paix." Lane's eyes were red. "What have you done?"

Suddenly, he felt ashamed. "It's best you don't know."

"We all make mistakes," Heap said, and the way he said it made Paix think that Heap spoke from experience, "but it doesn't have to ruin us."

Paix shook his head. "Reina didn't tell you?"

When Heap and Lane shook their heads, he said, "I'm in trouble with the Spadros Family."

Then he felt demoralized. How could he possibly survive?

"Oh, dear," Heap said, chagrined. But then he recovered. "To fall in fighting for a noble cause —"

Paix snorted. "Hardly noble. I've made a mess of it. But thank you for thinking well of me."

They ate in silence. And Paix pondered what Sheinwold had told him: the decision of his fate rested on the Spadros Heir.

While the character of the father was well-known, less was known of the son. What punishment would the man choose?

After dinner, Lane came to Paix and said, "We need to talk."

So he followed her out, and they sat on her front steps watching the carriages go by.

"Reina told me what she said to you, and I think you have the wrong impression."

This was interesting. "In what way?"

"When I was seventeen, my father betrothed me to an old man. His wife had died without an heir and I suppose he thought I was an improvement. But while I liked the man well enough, the thought of marrying him didn't appeal to me."

"I imagine not."

"Soon after that I went to the Plaza. A man my age sat knitting in a booth, and I asked my mother if I could watch him. I already knew how to knit, of course, but I'd never seen a man do it." Her cheeks colored. "He wasn't much more handsome than he is now, but he liked me, I could tell. No one had ever liked me before. As a woman."

"I'm sorry," Paix said.

"Don't be." She smiled. "I went to the booth every day. Turned out it belonged to his parents. He was shy at first, but we began to talk, and I'd bring my knitting. When my parents found out I was going there, they knew what was coming. They forbade me to visit. But Heap began sending notes and flowers. He said he'd never had anyone look at him like I did." She put her elbows on her knees, her chin in her hands. "I chose Heap Tableau because I love him, Paix, even though my parents disowned me. I couldn't live without him."

"Even though he's a Bridger?"

"Yes, he's a Bridger. And yes, he knows, or at least suspects, that I'm not. But we love each other. It makes it better that we have six children who love us, and that his parents left us the booth. Yet I'd be happy to spend my life with him even if we'd never had any of it."

She took a deep breath, let it out. "What you have to ask yourself is whether you can live without Reina. Whether you'd be happy to spend your life with her even if her husband never releases her." She put her hand on his knee. "Even," she looked him in the eye, "if it means you never have a child."

Paix stared at the ground. *Never have a child.* "I want her to be with me because she wants to, that's all."

"Well, I've held more than a few women who've had a tiff with their husband as they wept. She loves you. She wants to be with you. She's given up everything for you." She patted his knee. "Just think about what truly matters to you."

Paix didn't go back inside: instead, he returned home. He expected his rooms to be ransacked as Sheinwold's had been, but they hadn't been touched.

Paix sat on the edge of his bed, unable to sleep. What game did they play here? How long did he have to live?

* * *

The next morning, not knowing what else to do, Paix set off

159

for the station. Since the Trainees were off their assignments and the new ones wouldn't begin until Monday, he rode into the station alone.

The pre-shift briefing was uneventful. C.K. wouldn't look Paix in the eye.

Sheinwold's replacement, a fat, balding man with thick round spectacles which reminded Paix of carriage-driver's goggles, had evidently failed his physical fitness exams. He'd been banished to Precinct 1 until he could prove he was fit to return. But he and C.K. seemed instant friends, and the two went off after the briefing chattering away about cases.

So Paix and Briscola went on their beat, separating to do their own patrols. Paix was almost through his 1st Street house search when a messenger boy met him. "Detective Senior Constable Kanhu says he needs you back at the station at once."

Paix returned to the beat station to find Briscola waiting there for the wagon, having been summoned as well. By the time they arrrived at the precinct station, C.K. had gathered a dozen other Probationaries, dressed in their street clothes. "We just got word of a meet-up happening with our suspect and another man we believe to be directing his activities by the Statue after luncheon. We're to go there in twos, blend in with the crowd, and capture them both." He brandished Crab's portrait. "Do not approach the suspect until the signal. Understand?"

Briscola said, "What's the signal?"

C.K. pulled a dog whistle from his pocket. "The suspect will meet with our target. When the dogs start barking, move in."

It was an ingenious plan. The tourists invariably had their dogs with them on promenade, as did many of the Families. Yet this didn't expose C.K. as the source of the whistle.

"All right, men," C.K. said with a grin, "let's have luncheon."

Paix and Briscola decided to take the wagon to the beat station, walk to the Promenade, and take a police wagon the rest of the way, stopping off thirty yards before the Statue. They found a street vendor on the wharf side selling tamales, so they settled there at a table to eat. Paix relaxed into his chair with a smile. "Today, fine sir, we're in Precinct Zero!"

Briscola said, "You think this guy's really gonna show?"

Paix shrugged. From what Sheinwold had said, the young man was probably dead by now, or wishing he was. The Spadros Family didn't get to where it was by kind and gentle treatment.

"Well, well, well," a voice said. "Fancy seeing you here."

A flash of terror. Paix closed his eyes with a sigh. "Eight Howell. So they sent **you**."

21

Howell sat beside Paix. "I hope you're well."

Briscola's face was white, his eyes wide with fear.

"As well as can be expected," Paix said, hoping his voice wasn't shaking as badly as it sounded. "And you?"

"I'm not here to kill you," Howell said. "To be perfectly honest, I'm surprised to see you in Spadros quadrant at all. But I did always say you had more courage than the whole lot of them."

"That's very kind."

"Of course, now I'm beginning to wonder if it's that you're the stupidest man alive. Did you really do what they claim?"

Paix grimaced, his eyes flickering towards Briscola. "I'd really rather not speak of it here."

Howell leaned back. "Very well. But just so you know, our next talk may not be so pleasant if we meet in Spadros quadrant."

"I understand."

Howell rose. "And by the way, if you see your friends, tell them to leave the matter at the Statue to us." He glanced around. "Your people are anything but subtle." He tipped his cap. "Good day, Constables."

After he left, Briscola gulped. "So what do we do now?"

"We sit here," Paix said, "and watch the show."

* * *

Traffic was heavy, and several carriages resembling taxis but rather sporting black horses drove among the throng. Across the tree-lined street, Crab walked past, a red handkerchief dangling from his left jacket pocket. He continued on to the Statue, crossed the street, and stood there staring up at the monument.

Briscola said, "What does a guy like that think about?"

"Probably what everyone else does," Paix said.

Crab stood there quite a while. But no one approached him, and eventually he left, disappearing into the crowd.

C.K. jogged across the street towards them, his partner standing on the other side. "What are you two doing here?"

"The operation was blown," Paix said. "A Family man came by and warned us to stay put. What happened with you?"

"I put guys on him but the Family snapped him up."

"Pity," Paix said. "What do we do now?"

"There's a shootout in Diamond," C.K. said. "Been going on a while now. Want to come along?"

So C.K. flagged down a police wagon as his partner made his way across the street, and they all rode to the Diamond bridge.

But when they got out to approach the guard tower, several Diamond Associates stood there, big burly men with dark skin. "We've got it under control."

C.K. smirked. "Are you certain?"

At this, the man frowned. "We're certain."

A taxi-carriage came past going the other way, a brief glimpse of a maid's cap in the window.

"Very well," C.K. said. "But don't complain next time if we don't arrive when you call."

They returned to the station. When they got out of the wagon, C.K. hung back. "Thanks for what you did yesterday."

Paix shrugged. "We all have our bad days."

C.K. snorted. "That we do." He trudged up the steps, Paix following.

Paix said, "That new guy working out for you?"

C.K. considered this. "Yeah. He is." He seemed more cheerful than he'd been in a while.

As Paix passed the front desk, the clerk said, "The Commander wants to see you yesterday."

At this, Paix felt alarmed. "Whatever for?"

"I don't know," the clerk said, "but he's not happy."

When Paix walked in, the Commander was pacing in front of his desk. Paix said, "Reporting as requested, Commander."

"In all my days, I have never seen such a display of folly." He stopped pacing. "What were you thinking?"

"The woman destroyed those letters, I'm sure of —"

"So you found nothing, is that right? And cost us the regard of the entire quadrant. For what? Another hunch?"

Paix stared straight ahead. "Yes, Commander."

"And why did you not secure permission before interviewing Mrs. Spadros?"

"Permission? From who?"

"Her husband, you dolt! Who else do you think? He had no idea we'd been questioning her."

This left Paix shocked. Why, then, was he let in? And why had the butler not told her husband of the visits?

"You're the luckiest man alive, do you know that?"

"I'm not sure how to respond to that, Commander."

"Instead of having you killed, or sent to Roy Spadros, our Heir has granted you mercy."

Paix blinked. "Commander?"

"You're to be demoted to Probationary —"

"But —"

"— and transferred to Market Center. You're not to set foot in Spadros quadrant again. Ever. And you have two weeks suspension without pay."

Paix gaped at him. In one blow, their income had just been cut in half. "How will we survive?"

Commander Green scowled. "The nerve of you, Hanger! You've escaped death, or worse! Yet you complain. For falsely prosecuting a warrant, I could have you dismissed and brought up on Federal charges! Would you rather that?"

He felt abashed. "No, Commander."

"Neither does anyone involved. But you should have considered the consequences before you intruded on the man's home without leave, questioned his wife — twice — without leave, assaulted his servant, and vandalized his property. Would you rather die? Accept your fate, and you may yet have a future!"

"Damn Spadros," Paix muttered.

The Commander stopped then, facing him. "I don't know what you have against this man. I've watched him since he was born, and he's not his father. Anthony Spadros is just trying to protect his wife, his people, and his property. The fact he feels need to do so from us is abominable!"

"But he's a criminal —"

"And when we have means to bring him to trial, we'll do so. Until then, we must follow the law! Or we're no better than he is."

Paix had nothing to say to that.

"I need your badge."

Paix unpinned it from his hat and handed it over.

"You're dismissed. Go home. Report to Market Center station two weeks from today."

"Yes, Commander."

Paix stumbled out, not hearing Briscola calling after him, feeling numb.

A hand fell on his shoulder: Briscola's. "What's going on?"

"I'm done," Paix said. "Reassigned Probationary on Market Center."

Briscola grabbed Paix by the shoulders. "Why? What happened?"

"You don't want to know." Paix looked away, eyes stinging. "You shouldn't be seen with me."

"They can go fuck themselves," Briscola said. "Let's get you home."

* * *

After the wagon dropped him off at the Market Center station, Paix trudged to his empty room.

How could he continue to work like this?

He lay on top of the covers on his bed, still dressed, staring at the ceiling. He was still alive.

Maybe he could find David Bryce. Maybe he could learn who took him. Thunder cracked, and outside, the rain began to fall.

The next day, Paix got up, put on his uniform, and took the wagon alone in the pouring rain into Spadros quadrant. No one challenged him. He got off at the Precinct 8 station on 190th and Snow then walked, umbrella in hand, to Spadros Manor.

Last he heard, Crab was being questioned at the Manor.

Maybe Crab was still there.

Maybe he was still alive.

Maybe he knew something.

Paix walked up to the Manor; a coroner's wagon stood by. Several men watched as a body was being carried out. Blood soaked one end of the sheets where the head should've been.

Did the Family murder him? Horrified, Paix said without meaning to, "What happened?"

One of the men glanced over. A young man, twenty or so, with straight black hair and blue eyes, holding a black umbrella. "Killed himself." He sounded weary, regretful. "I suppose he couldn't bear what he'd done."

The coroner's men lay the body beside another one already in the wagon.

Paix peered at the young man standing beside him. *This is the Spadros Heir.*

But this Anthony Spadros seemed a different man than the hard-faced thug in the news portraits, as if some mask had been washed away by his grief.

He's barely more than a boy.

And some core of bitterness and hate broke, softened. *He's just trying to protect his people.* "I'm truly sorry for your loss," Paix said, and he meant it. "Let us know how we can help."

At that, Anthony Spadros nodded slowly, eyes downcast, grief-stricken, and turned away.

One of the coroner's men said, "You want a lift back to the station, Constable?"

"Yes, thank you."

In the downpour, no one asked questions, and Paix made it back to Market Center station without any trouble. As he got out of the wagon, Commander Green emerged from the station, umbrella in hand. Their eyes met, and Green began to laugh as he stood under the eaves.

Paix walked to him, closing his umbrella when he arrived. "What are you doing here?"

"Just couldn't resist going back one last time, eh?"

"I suppose, Commander." Then Paix had a flash of insight

which humbled him: *he's believed in me this entire time.* "You were right. About the Heir."

Commander Green gave Paix a startled glance, and Paix nodded. The two stood watching the rain.

Paix could have left then, walked home, but he felt that the Commander still wished to say something to him.

Commander Green finally said, "I've resigned."

"What?" Green had been in the force longer than anyone!

"Your little escapade had consequences," Green said. "They put Pattsz in charge." He shook his head, and the deep raspy cough returned. When he recovered, he said, "I still believe our best hope is working with the Families to improve the city." At that, he seemed encouraged. "But I can do better work elsewhere."

"Where will you go?"

At that, he grinned, and looked like a man ten years younger. "My cousin runs the Clubb desk at the *Bridges Daily*. He's secured me a position."

"Well," Paix said, impressed. "Congratulations! I wish you all the best."

A quadrant-wagon pulled up. Reporter Wolff Green got into it and closed the door behind him.

As the wagon pulled away, a taxi-carriage stopped across the street. Briscola got out, raised his coat over his head, and ran through the downpour. "Did you hear? They found the boy."

Paix gasped. "Who found him? Where?"

Briscola shook his head. "The mother won't talk; I think she's protecting whoever found him."

Paix considered this. "Crab's dead."

Briscola gaped at him.

Paix nodded. "Suicide."

He couldn't bear what he'd done.

What **had** Crab done?

He clapped Briscola on the shoulder. "Congratulations. And give my regards to Kanhu. Your case is closed."

"But I thought you didn't think Crab took David Bryce."

"I still don't. Take credit for your part in it anyway. You hear? You helped solve a multiple murder-kidnapping case. When you've done your six months, put it at the top of your request to transfer. I don't want you to be in Precinct 1 an instant longer than need be."

They'd come close, so the true villain would probably lay low for a while. *If he likes strangling, he's not going to stop until we stop him.* By the time this scoundrel began killing again, Paix wanted Briscola out of Precinct 1 and the coming storm of recriminations. As the Detective Senior Constable on record, it was too late for C.K. But maybe Briscola would survive.

Briscola nodded. "I understand."

"You know Howell now, so Precinct 2 shouldn't be too difficult for you. Look him up as soon as you transfer over. Sooner, if you like. Learn to play the game." Paix grinned. "I expect great things from you."

Briscola's cheeks reddened. "Thank you, Constable."

"That's Probationary Constable to you," Paix said cheerfully.

He'd come to terms with it in the coroner's wagon as he squatted beside Crab's bloody corpse. Coming so close to torture and death made him realize he was grateful to the young man who'd spared him.

Why Anthony Spadros let him live, he'd never know. But Paix planned to make the most of it.

He would learn who kidnapped that boy, who murdered those others. He would find this woman Eunice Ogier. He would bring the men responsible to justice, if it took him the rest of his life.

Paix patted Briscola on the shoulder, opened his umbrella, and walked towards Lane's house to get Reina. It was safe for them to go home.

Want to know what really happened?
Who found David?
Who Eunice Ogier is, and what she's doing?

Drawing Thin is a companion to the
Red Dog Conspiracy steampunk noir crime fiction series,
which begins with Part 1: *The Jacq of Spades*.

Learn more at JacqOfSpades.com.

About the Author

Patricia Loofbourrow, MD is a NY Times and USA Today best-selling science fiction writer, PC gamer, ornamental food gardener, fiber artist, and wildcrafter who loves power tools, dancing, genetics and anything to do with outer space. She was born in southern California and currently lives in Oklahoma with her husband and three grown children.

Acknowledgments

Thanks to Margaret Fisk for beta reading this book, and to my street team, The Commission, for helping to get it into your hands.
Special thanks to my Patrons: without your monthly financial donations, this paperback edition would not have been possible:

Melissa Williams

Julian White

Michaelene Alston

Cristina

Eirlys Evans

Jane Kavmar

Rachel Heslin

Phoebe Darqueling

Dave Kobrenski

Follow the Red Dog Conspiracy on Patreon
patreon.com/red_dog_conspiracy

9 781944 223274